DEADLY DIRECTION

A BRITANNIA BAY MYSTERY

SYDNEY PRESTON

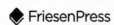

FriesenPress

One Printers Way
Altona, MB R0G 0B0
Canada

www.friesenpress.com

ISBN
978-1-03-914158-2 (Hardcover)
978-1-03-914157-5 (Paperback)
978-1-03-914159-9 (eBook)

1. *FICTION, MYSTERY & DETECTIVE, COZY, GENERAL*

Distributed to the trade by The Ingram Book Company

CAST OF PERMANENT CHARACTERS IN THE SERIES

DETECTIVE SERGEANT JIMMY TAN
Wife, Ariel

ROSSINI FAMILY
Detective Sergeant Ray Rossini
Wife, Georgina
Children, Marcus and Gabriella
Umberto and Silvana Rossini, Ray's parents and owners of Catalani's Italian Ristorante

BRITANNIA BAY POLICE DEPARTMENT

CHIEF WILLIAM WYATT. WIFE, SHERILEE
Detective Sergeant and SOCO, Josh Atkins
Constables: Adam Berry, Craig Carpenter, Dalbir Dhillon, Tamsyn Foxcroft, Mike Heppner, Gene McDaniel, Tim Novak, Simon Rhys-Jones
Special Municipal Constable and Media Liaison, Marina Davidova
Dispatchers, Mary Beth McKay, Robyn Lewitski

R.C.M.P.
Corporal Ike Griffin*

CORONER/MEDICAL OFFICER
Dr. Dayani Nayagam

BRITANNIA BAY RESIDENTS
Clive Abernathy, President of Heritage Gardens Society. He and his wife Daphne, own Charterhouse B&B
Justine Hughes, owner of Justine's Joint café
Keith Kittridge, editor of *The Bayside Bugle*. Wife, Edith
Delilah Moore, neighbour of the Tans
Pieter Verhagen, Mayor
Lana Westbrook, neighbour of the Tans and Pastry Chef for Catalani's**

---

* Corporal Griffin has been a major figure in the first two books in the series. He does not, however, appear in "Deadly Direction." He will be returning.

** Lana Westbrook has also been an important person in the series, but she may or may not return.

"Screw your courage to the sticking place."

Macbeth
William Shakespeare

Prologue

Where is it? Where did it go? For what seemed like the hundredth time, he searched everything, everywhere, even looking inside the luggage lining, although certain it wouldn't be there. Someone had slipped it in his jacket pocket. But who? And when? And where? And what did it mean? *Watch Your Back!* Why did he have to watch his back?

He sat at the dainty desk on a delicate chair and went over the list once again. Who would have done it? He didn't know most of the crew from Vancouver. Or did he? Did any of them work with him ten years ago? They seemed too young. And why would they warn him? No. He was sure it wasn't one of them. Which meant …

It was time to go downstairs for breakfast. First, he had to double check that he had locked his valise. He was forgetting too many things these days. Yes. The gun was safe. But was he?

One

Tuesday, October 21st

Mayor Pieter Verhagen listened with limited patience as yet another request–more like a demand–was being asked of him. When the townsfolk heard that a television show from Hollywood would be locating in Britannia Bay, they had been gripped with excitement. But Verhagen was already fed up. After only two weeks, the head honcho seemed to regard it as just another Hollywood set. "Mr. Benson, please understand that the town has already allowed you to transform the Tourist Information Centre into a house. The path beside it is regularly used by residents. We can't have it blocked off all day."

Allen Benson frowned. He hadn't planned on any kind of pushback from this small town mayor. After all *Paradise Pines* was a successful television production and he should be bending over backwards to accommodate them. "The thing is, we have to set up a dolly track. This isn't something you just lay down and pick up at a moment's notice," he said tetchily. "It takes time to lay the track and it has to stay in place until the scene is shot. We can't have people stumbling over it. That's why we need more cones and tape … to keep people away from the area. And we need at least one police officer present to make sure they keep their distance."

Verhagen's stomach did a flip. He knew what Chief Wyatt's reaction would be to that request. "How much time are we looking at here?"

"We'll need the morning to get the track set up and the lighting equipment in place. We're looking to shoot between one and three in the afternoon. So the pathway would be unavailable all day."

Verhagen blanched. "And this would be for two days only?"

"The script calls for two days. But you never know. If there's a glitch, we may need another day. It depends on the weather."

"This rain is expected to stop later today. And we're looking forward to a week of sunshine."

"Yes, I know that," Benson said through gritted teeth.

But Verhagen knew that bay area weather forecasts were doled out along with a hope and a prayer. "We'll provide more cones and tape and put up warning signs. I'll call the police chief to see what we can do about getting one constable."

Benson stood. "Well, if that's all you can do, we'll just have to make the best of it." He wheeled around, leaving without another word.

Verhagen sighed. He knew that the citizens were pleased to have a Hollywood production shooting in their little community, but he also knew how wedded the seniors were to their habits. Cutting through that pathway from their medical appointments on Church Street to their refreshments at Justine's Joint was as ingrained in them as an animal's instincts.

Chief of Police William Wyatt longed to slam down the phone on a receiver but that kind of dramatic gesture was no longer possible. Swearing, he flung it onto his desk sending it skittering along the top and onto the floor. Glowering, he turned to his computer. Grumbling, he scrolled through his folders, opening up the shift roster. Even though he knew the present marital relationships of all his constables, he still ran through it trying to decide which poor sap was going to get the assignment. He sighed. It had to be J.D. Dussault. She was the one with the lowest rank and, from all the bits and pieces of flotsam floating around the station, he had fashioned the current picture of her personal life.

Janice Delphine was still living the single life after the Berdahl murder a couple of years before. That case had galvanized her determination to dedicate her life to police work, resulting in her partner's decision to leave her.

Wyatt observed that J.D. had done a damn fine job, and he tried to show his appreciation, shouldering her with more and serious responsibilities. But there was little room for movement on the team–unless someone chose to resign. He contemplated firing Frank "loose lips" Paulson, but knew the little creep would run to the Labour Relations Board and Wyatt wouldn't have much of a leg to stand on. You couldn't put down "gossiping" and "trouble maker" as a reason to fire someone. Not these days.

He looked through the windows of his office into the squad room–a large open area containing eight shared work stations. Dussault was among those in attendance, but his attention was drawn to Constables Tamsyn Foxcroft and Craig Carpenter. They were nose-to-nose in an apparent heated discussion. Everyone else was smiling. Wyatt decided to check it out. Quietly stepping through his doorway, he heard: "If white people didn't buy them, we wouldn't need to sell them. It's you people who are causing all the trouble!"

Since the first mention of Hallowe'en in the media, illegal fireworks had been a topic of conversation at the station. The police were constantly called out to arrest someone in violation of the sale, usually someone who had purchased large quantities from one of the local First Nations bands, of which Foxcroft was a member.

Wyatt entered their workspace. The immediate silence from the other constables alerted Foxcroft and Carpenter that the boss was present. They straightened up and tried to look like law enforcement personnel, not rabble rousers.

He held up one hand. "You can continue that after I've dealt with an issue that's landed in our laps. I got a call from our beloved mayor with a request. Seems that the producer of *Paradise Pines* wants some police presence around one of his locations. Warning cones and signs aren't enough for him. He wants someone to direct people away from the taped-off area."

"What area are we talking about, Chief?" Detective Sergeant Ray Rossini asked.

"Around the Tourist Information Centre. They're turning that into a cottage."

"That's not going to be so easy," D.S. Jimmy Tan said. "The pathway beside it is a convenient short-cut between all the clinics and the grocery store, not to mention Justine's."

Wyatt nodded. "The mayor has suggested we have one constable on the Church Street side. He'll have traffic cones and warning signs as well."

"So who's the lucky cop that gets this plum assignment?" Carpenter piped up.

Wyatt ignored him and looked at Dussault. "Sorry, J.D. But you're low man on the totem pole, so it looks like it's going to be you."

As J.D. was replying to Wyatt, Carpenter whispered in Foxcroft's ear. "Correct pronoun, I believe."

She looked at him sharply.

When Dussault followed Wyatt back to his office, Foxcroft seized Carpenter's arm in a vise-like grip. "If you ever make a homophobic comment about her again, I will personally rip this arm off you. Got that? I don't give a shit about your racist comments about my people, but I won't stand for you dissing someone as nice and hard-working as J.D."

Her words were quiet but picked up by a few of the officers. Since they had been partnered during the homicide two years before, Foxcroft had reined in Carpenter's penchant for acting like a horse's ass. But every once in a while, the horse got away. His face turned red. That was enough for Foxcroft. She dropped her hand and went to her desk, more disappointed than angry.

Two

Annika Johansson spread butter on toast and went to the fridge for jam. While her back was turned, Sara, her seven-year-old daughter, took advantage of the moment to surreptitiously drop some hard-cooked egg white on the floor. Maisie, the beagle, watching from her corner bed, made a beeline for it.

"Sara … " Annika admonished her.

"What?"

"Oh, don't go all innocent on me, young lady. You know exactly what you were doing. You were giving your food to Maisie."

"How did you know?" Sara whined.

Maisie, recognizing the pattern of sounds, crept back to her bed in the corner.

"I keep telling you that I have special eyes."

"I don't see them," Sara challenged her.

"You're not supposed to see them, you silly goose. That's why they're special."

"How come you have special eyes?"

"Because all Swedish people have special heads. And don't you say they're square, like your dad does!" Annika cautioned.

"Not if I value my life," Sara said, repeating one of his favourite lines.

Annika burst out laughing. Then the laugh softened into a sad smile. Sara went silent. They missed Zack. She looked at the clock, then turned up the volume on the radio.

"*Coming up on the eight o'clock news, an update on the flooding across the province. But first these messages …*"

She turned down the volume. "Finish your egg, Sara, and not just the yoke."

"The white part hasn't got any taste."

"It's still very good for you. Even Maisie knows that."

"Maisie'll eat anything."

Annika turned up the volume as the urgent voice of the broadcaster updated listeners with the latest news, news that had become an integral part of her and Sara's lives. As she attuned her ears to the most important part of the broadcast, the phone rang.

"*Oh, damn!* Hello!" she answered the phone sharply.

"Hi, babe," Zack's deep voice resonated in her ear. "You sounded a bit testy just then." He chuckled.

"Oh, honey! It's you. I was just waiting to hear more about the flooding and the mudslide." Annika sank into a chair.

"Daddy!" Sara yelled, jumping down from the table, tipping her egg cup onto the floor. Maisie was on it in a flash.

"I'll put on the speaker phone so that Sara can hear you."

"I have to make this pretty quick. It's a massive slide that's covering the highway, so we're being directed to a holding place. I thought I'd call while I had the chance. I just wanted to tell you that I'm okay."

"Hi, Daddy!" Sara chimed in.

"Hi, sweetie. How are you?"

"We're making Hallowe'en costumes."

"That sounds like fun. What are you going to be?"

"A fairy. Will you be here for Hallowe'en?"

"Right now, I don't know. I'm sorry. The road is closed and I don't know when it'll be open."

"You've been gone a long time. I miss playing with you."

"I know. I'm sorry about that, too."

"That's okay. Ariel's going to get me today. We do things, but they're not as fun as what me and you do."

"Well you know, she's not a mechanic."

Sara giggled. "I'm learning about bees."

"Bees are good, too. And they won't sting you if you don't bother them."

"That's what she said."

"I have to make this a fast call, sweetie, so I need to talk to your mom again. Okay?"

Deflated, she hesitated. "Okay, but will you phone again?"

"As soon as I get a chance. Remember, I love you … big time."

"I love you too, Daddy. Big time."

"God, we miss you," Annika said. "Six weeks is a long time."

He sighed. "It was the best decision. The only one. You know that. It won't be like this forever. I'm hoping to hear from that airline company. They said they would notify me when they had an opening."

"But that would mean we would have to move again."

"Probably."

"Well, it's a good idea that I've finally decided to home school Sara. That way there won't be any more disruptions."

"She's resilient. I wouldn't worry about our girl. By the way, have you checked the bank balance lately?"

"I did it yesterday."

"Pretty nice having all of that dough-re-mi, isn't it?"

"Yes, but I'd rather have you." She tried to keep the pleading out of her voice. "I guess you won't be home soon."

"It doesn't look that way right now. There's no telling when they'll get this mudslide cleared. Apparently half the hillside came down."

"I know. The news is full of it."

"I'll be home the minute I get a chance. Keep texting me, okay?"

"I will." She heard talking in the background.

"I gotta go, honey."

"Okay. *Jag älskar dig, hjärtat.*"

"And I love you, too, sweetheart." And he was gone.

Annika looked at the phone as though it were nothing but a bearer of bad news. All she wanted to do was sit and have a good cry, but life was getting in the way of that.

"Don't be sad, Mom. I'll be your *hjärtat.*"

Annika crouched and gathered Sara in her arms hugging her hard. "Oh, you wonderful little girl! You'll always be my sweetheart!"

Maisie wanted to get in on the hug and wedged herself between them, her backside whipping back and forth like a metronome on *presto*. They laughed. The blue mood was broken. Annika glanced at the clock. "We have to get moving or we're going to be late. Go and brush your teeth while I clean up the kitchen."

By the time Annika picked up the eggcup and wiped up the mess, Sara had returned. "Get your rain slicker and gumboots and put your shoes in your backpack while I get myself ready," Annika said. "And give Maisie some treats."

The little beagle sat, expectant, as Sara reached into a canister, took out several treats and placed them on the floor. "That's all until I get home," she told her. Maisie scoffed down the cookies, content for now. Sara was dressed and ready when Annika came back in, fastening her rain jacket over her sweater and the vest from Helen's Hardware.

"Okay, let's hit the streets, kiddo."

As they turned from the lane beside their house onto Forsythia Street, they saw Ariel Tan under a large red and white umbrella, a hold-over from Canada Day, when it rained on the parade. She was lowering the lid on a recycle bin.

"Good morning, Ariel."

"Hi, Annika."

"What are you doing out here? Isn't that Jimmy's job?" she laughed.

"He always takes them out before I've put in last-minute things."

"Can you believe this rain?"

"Hi, Ariel." Sara skipped up to her.

"Hi, Sara. You look very cheerful in your yellow outfit," she greeted her. "It brightens up the day."

"I especially like my yellow gumboots."

"Yes, I wouldn't mind a pair like that myself." She turned back to Annika. "It's a real downpour isn't it? You wonder when it's going to stop. The cats are even cranky," she laughed.

Sara was twirling around, dancing to silent music spinning somewhere in her little head. "We get out at two o'clock today," she dutifully reminded Ariel.

"Yes, I know. I'll be there."

"Thanks for doing this, Ariel. You're an angel. Helen's letting me off work so that I can go to the meeting. It should be over by three o'clock … unless some parents want to put in their two-cents' worth."

"Really, I don't mind at all. It's a pleasure." And it *was* a pleasure. Sara was curious, creative and remarkably compassionate for one so young. Ariel enjoyed every moment in her company. Right now she enjoyed watching her pummeling a puddle with her little yellow boots.

"Are we going to the Library today?" Sara asked.

"Yes, we'll do that and if it's okay with your mother, we'll go to Justine's for some goodies after."

"Is it okay with you, Mommy?"

"Of course. I'll join you after the meeting." Annika pointed to her watch behind her daughter's back.

Ariel got the hint. "I'll wait for you at the usual place, Sara."

"See you later, Ariel. Come on, Sara," she said, urging her along. Impatient, she grabbed the girl's hand and strode down the street, Sara's little legs struggling to keep up.

A grating sound from across the street caught Ariel's attention. Delilah Moore, their elderly neighbour, was pulling a garbage bin along her concrete driveway. Ariel dashed over. "Here, Lilah. Let me do that. Hold my umbrella."

"Thank you, Ariel. Either those bins are getting heavier or I'm getting weaker. But it must be the latter because I throw about the same amount of stuff in them every couple of weeks." She stood under the oversized umbrella watching how easily Ariel pushed the bin out to the street.

"Do you have any recycling?"

"Not this week. It's only got a couple of soup cans and unread *Bugles* in it. I don't know why I bother to take it. The only way I can read it is with my magnifying glass. And half the time I can't find that. I'm only interested in the obituaries anyway." She laughed. "One day soon I'll be reading my own."

"You're being silly, Lilah. You have more energy than people half your age."

"That's only after I get going. And that's taking longer than usual, too."

"You'd better get in out of the rain. I'll walk you to your door."

The old lady threaded her arm through Ariel's and walked with an unsteady gait to the front door. Ariel could feel the pressure on her arm. She knew that, without her walker, Delilah could easily lose her footing, and fall. It had happened a couple of years back and landed her in the hospital with a broken wrist.

"Thank you, dear," she said, upon reaching her porch.

Tabitha, Delilah's tortoise-shell cat, was sitting on the back of the couch watching everything with her green eyes. When the door opened she jumped down. Delilah bent over and petted her cat a couple of times. "I wasn't gone more than a minute, Tabitha." She straightened up and looked at Ariel. "She's such good company. Gives me a reason to get up and get to my day. Everybody should have a pet if they don't have children."

As she walked back across the street, Ariel agreed with her. That's why we have two, she said to herself. But she often had to be reminded that Molly and Roger were not children, but cats.

Three

Georgina Rossini was in a state of euphoria gazing at Catalani's refurbished kitchen. "I can't believe the difference, Mamma," she said to her mother-in-law, Silvana, the *materfamilias* of the Rossini clan. "Look at how much room we have now."

"*Si. Es el cielo,*" Silvana replied, pointing to the ceiling.

"It was Providence that the space next door became available."

"*Mala suerte para ella. Buena suerte para nosotros,*" she commented dryly.

"Bad luck. Good luck. Whatever. *She* was happy to get a buyer and *we* were fortunate to have the money."

Into this conversation stepped Lana Westbrook, their Paris-trained *maître pâtissier*, dragging a covered serving cart behind her. After greeting everyone, she removed and hung up her Burberry trench coat and then got busy placing two trays of double chocolate biscotti, a ganache-topped chocolate gateau and two Amalfi lemon cakes into one of the massive refrigerators. The pastries came from her own restaurant-style kitchen in a house she had had gutted and refurbished upon arriving in Britannia Bay six years before. All the while, the eyes of Stefano Moretti, the new Italian sous chef from Pesaro, followed her.

Silvana traced their path. Something was going on, all right. Georgina had mentioned it.

"You know, Mamma, I'm sure something happened in Pesaro when Lana came to visit us because he clearly has a thing for her. When she arrives, he almost stops what he's doing and watches her. But I haven't seen any response from Lana. At least, not yet."

Silvana took notice of how Lana was taking extra time, hovering beside Gabriella, the youngest member of the family, who was busy piping filling into cannoli shells.

"Are you here again?" Lana said to Gabriella, laughing as she dipped a spoon into the zesty mixture.

"I didn't have any classes this afternoon."

"Did you make this filling?"

"Uh-huh. What do you think?"

Lana tasted it and nodded. ""It's perfect. The patrons are going to swoon with all these choices, Gabby."

"One of these days I'm going to tackle the *torta setteveli*."

"Then they'll really swoon," Lana said.

"Too bad we don't have someone like Salome to dance the seven veils while it's being served." She giggled.

"Well, you could get the staff to wiggle their rear ends and wave around some napkins." As she said this, she snatched up a napkin, waved it around, wiggled her tall, slim body in a sensuous dance, and hummed what she considered to be a snippet of the "Bacchanale" from *Samson and Delilah*.

Mouths dropped open. It was *so* out of character for Lana, or so most of them thought. Only Stefano had witnessed Lana's mischievous side during their secret trip from Pesaro to Paris. He laughed and applauded. "Brava, signorina," he called out, promptly causing Lana to stop. She blushed. Dropping the napkin into a nearby laundry bin, she donned her coat and dragged her cart through the exit. Stefano watched with a trace of the lust in his eyes that Salome must have generated in King Herod. It was not lost on Silvana.

Ariel and Sara sat at a table in Justine's Joint having hot cocoa. "I like these little marshmallows, Ariel," Sara said. "They're like jelly pillows for forest fairies. When they wake up in the morning, they eat them for breakfast."

"But what do they do at night when they need pillows again?"

"Well, during the day, the elves make more. And they spread them around everywhere, so all the creatures of the forest can find one before they go to sleep. And they're all different colours. But the fairies like the white ones best," Sara explained with all the seriousness and conviction of a young child.

"Why do you think they like the white ones best?"

"Because white is the colour of angels' wings."

Ariel nodded. "That makes sense."

An elderly man wearing a wind-proof parka and heavy boots sat at the table next to them listening to their conversation. The earnestness of the little girl's words had a smile spreading into the creases of his weather-beaten face. She was obviously not the daughter of the woman with the light brown curls because she had addressed her by her name.

Ariel caught his eye. "What do you think? Does this make sense to you?" she asked him.

"Absolutely. I know if I were a fairy I would want a white pillow, but I would want it to glow with a bright light around the edges."

Sara stared at the man, wide-eyed. "That's right! Angels make them glow."

"And so do fairies when they fly into the air. They beat their wings and it generates light. Fairies are magical," he said seriously.

"I'm going to be a fairy on Hallowe'en night!" she bubbled over with enthusiasm.

"Well, I can already tell that you are not going to be an ordinary fairy. You're going to be a fairy *princess*."

Sara's mouth shaped into an O.

"And if you don't live too far away, you make sure you come to my house on Hallowe'en because I always have special treats for fairy princesses," he added.

"Where do you live?" Ariel asked.

"On the corner of Hyacinth and Maple."

"That's very close," Ariel said.

"Well, then. There's no excuse for you not coming. I always have a lot of decorations, so you can't miss it." He got up to leave.

"Goodbye Mister …" Sara began.

"Goodbody. Percy Goodbody. And it was nice to meet you, Fairy Princess." He rose then bent down and picked up a cloth shopping bag. He gave a little wave as he walked out.

"He's nice man," Sara said.

Ariel agreed.

Percy walked toward Off Yer Rockers, grateful that the rain had stopped. As he approached the Tourist Centre where people were preparing the area for filming, he saw Delilah Moore coming his way, wrestling with her grocery-laden walker. At the taped-off pathway beside what was now a cottage, the front wheels caught on one of the cables delivering power to the light reflectors, jarring it to a stop. She lost her balance and was tilting to one side when Percy rushed up and grabbed her.

"Oof!" she gasped, hanging onto his arm. "These idiots haven't got a lick of sense! Putting obstructions in the way of pedestrians."

As he was about to comment, a crew member hurried over. "I'm sorry. Are you all right? Signs are up everywhere warning people to stay away from this area."

She fixed him with a withering gaze. "You are assuming everyone has twenty-twenty vision. Don't you know that most of the population of Britannia Bay is half blind!? And I'm one of them!"

"I apologize. But please try to stay away from this pathway for the next couple of days. We'll be out of here then."

"And not a moment too soon," she added.

As the man walked off, Percy grinned. He knew Delilah well. She would drop into Off Yer Rockers for a snack a couple of times a week. All action from his crib-playing cronies would stop in anticipation of her wisecracks. They were rarely disappointed.

She turned to him. "Did you know about this, Percy?"

"Yes. I read an article in the paper. But I thought you would know, being on that town committee and all." He pulled her walker over the offending cables.

She grasped the handles. "You're right. I do remember now. Guess I'm finally losing my marbles." She didn't want to admit that she wasn't able to easily read the paper anymore.

"Oh, I doubt that, Delilah. You're one of the sharpest knives in the drawer."

She cackled. "And you're full of hooey. Thanks for keeping me upright."

"I think I'm too late for that," he chuckled.

"Cheeky." Before trundling off, she told him she was going to complain to the mayor.

At Off Yer Rockers, Percy made his way to the table where his friends were busy with their cards and pegs. "Hey, Percy, you're just in time. We need another man so that this reprobate here can play."

He took in the assembled group. "Ah, so you're the culprit, eh, Greenwood?"

"You should greet your visitors more cordially, Percy."

"What brings you up this way, Gordon?"

"I got a call from that film company saying they wanted to rent a house I have listed. So I'm going to meet up with the man in a half hour or so. Thought I'd honour you with the pleasure of my company in the meantime."

As they concentrated on the cards, the talk turned to the town's reaction to the filming. Percy told them about Delilah's altercation with one of the crew, evoking some laughter.

"Say, Percy," Greenwood began. "Don't you live on Hyacinth Road?"

"I do. Why?"

"Well, the house I'm showing is on Hyacinth."

"You don't say. It must be the one at the corner of Larch. It's the only vacant house on the street."

"It is."

"Well, I just hope they don't throw any of those Hollywood orgies while they're here. We are respectful folks and don't go in for any shenanigans."

"Oh, I don't know," Jasper said. "I wouldn't mind going to an orgy before I die."

"I don't think Winnie would approve of that, Jasper."

The chuckles were a bit subdued knowing that Jasper's wife had just been confined to a wheelchair after suffering a stroke.

"I'd better get home to her. My neighbour was good enough to come in for an hour or so to keep her company and make sure nothing happened while I was gone."

As he got up to leave, Percy handed him the cloth bag. "These are for the weekend. Jasper. I know that Dinner At Your Doorstep doesn't deliver then."

"Much obliged, Percy. Their meals are good but have a tendency to taste the same, whether it's chicken or pork chops."

After a few more games, the men put away the boards, gathered up their coats and bade each other goodbye. One of the men punched Percy lightly on the arm. "You're a good man, Goodbody."

Four

After Annika arrived at Justine's Joint, Ariel left her and Sara and picked up some groceries, then stopped to get the mail. A few minutes after she hung up her coat, the doorbell rang. It was Delilah.

"Hi, Lilah. Come on in."

"I've come to ask you for a favour, Ariel."

"Okay. Shall I put on some water for tea?"

"No, thanks. I only need you to write a letter for me before it's out of my head and before you start getting dinner ready."

"Oh? Okay. Have a seat. I'll just be a second." She went back to the den for lined paper, returned to the kitchen, and got a pen from the jar on the kitchen counter.

"So, who is it to?"

"First let me tell you the circumstances." And she related the incident with the walker-snaring cable. "You know, I could have gone ass over teakettle. I had a good mind to go straight to the mayor, but then I got a better idea. I want you to write to the *Brickbats and Bouquets* section of *The Bayside Bugle* and tell them what a bunch of jackasses this Hollywood bunch are." She laughed. "Of course, not in so many words."

"I think between the two of us we'll come up with a civil way to say that. By the way, did you say that it was Percy Goodbody who came to your rescue?"

"Yes. Do you know him?"

"Not really. But it's so funny, as in funny strange. He was in Justine's this afternoon and he charmed the dickens out of Sara. He was listening to her explaining some things about fairies and elves and he joined right in and gave her words as much weight as if they were spoken by an adult. And you know Sara. She's such a bright little girl. For her to get vindication from a total stranger … well, she was almost lost for words, which would be impossible for her. Then he said she should be sure to come by his place on Hallowe'en and I found out he lives just a couple of blocks away on Hyacinth. And I've never even *seen* him before."

"That's because you're too young, Ariel. If you dropped in to Off Yer Rockers, you might see him."

"I didn't think you went there because it was for old folks."

Delilah pursed her lips before answering. "Well, between you and me and the gatepost, I drop in once in a while because they have really good sandwiches and desserts and a decent cup of coffee. And it's cheap. And except for a few screwballs, the people are fun."

Ariel nodded. "Sounds like a nice place to spend some time."

"Yes. Now, let's get to that letter."

Percy was finishing his dinner when the phone rang. Looking at the display, he picked up. "Thanks for returning my call, Jade."

"What time would you like to come tomorrow, Percy?"

"What time would suit you?"

"I'll start picking those Ambrosias around eight o'clock. So anytime around then is fine."

"Okay. You said you didn't need another ladder. Are you sure?"

"Yes, I'm sure. I've got all the equipment I need. Just need another pair of hands."

"Well, you've got 'em, Jade. See you tomorrow."

Jimmy Tan polished off the prawns with garlic and ginger, and put on the kettle. "Do you want green tea, Ariel? You usually do after Thai food. And by the way, that was mighty fine grub, ma'am."

She laughed at his imitation of John Wayne. "You're such a clown. And yes, and thank y'all." She began removing the plates. "I wonder if Delilah's letter will make it into this week's *Brickbats and Bouquets*. I hope so."

"It probably will. Kittridge needs something to fill up his pages. Britannia Bay doesn't generate much news. And that's a popular column—that and the obituaries."

"I had quite a time getting her words into something printable, not that she used any profanity."

"No. She wouldn't, being a Christian. The most you'd get out of her would be dagnabit."

"She called them jackasses."

Jimmy laughed. "She's a real screwball."

Long after the town rolled up its sidewalks, leaving the streets to skateboarders, Silvana and her husband, Umberto, were lying in bed discussing Lana and Stefano.

"Georgina is right, Silvana. We can't do anything about it. They are two adults. As long as it doesn't upset the running of the restaurant, we shouldn't interfere. When he goes back to Italy, it will sort itself out."

"But what if she gets it in her head that it will be more than a flirtation for him … that perhaps there's a future with him? You know what Italian men are like … full of flowery words that don't mean a thing. I like her and I wouldn't want to see her get hurt. And another thing. What do we know about him other than what our crazy daughter told us? She's such an idiot when it comes to men. He shows up in Pesaro at her trattoria looking for work, she sees a handsome face, and her brain hits the pause button. For all we know, he could be a gangster on the run."

Umberto burst out laughing. 'You're watching too many crime shows on TV."

"We don't even know if he's from Torino."

"He's fluent in the dialect."

She ignored him. "And you know, Lana Westbrook comes from wealth. Real wealth. She attended the Institut Villa Pierrefeu in Switzerland. That kind of finishing school doesn't come cheap. Don't think he doesn't know that. She looks like money. She even *smells* like money."

He snorted. "Now I *know* you are watching silly dramas."

His words were not making any impact. She carried on. "Gabriella said Lana and Stefano spoke French in Pesaro," she said.

"That's another reason to believe he comes from Torino. They get a lot of French tourists. Especially in the winter when they come to ski. So it would be simple for him to pick up French."

"And another thing … did he really work for one of the diluted members of the House of Savoy? And why did he leave? Or did he get fired? And if he did, then why?"

Silvana remained silent for so long that when she suddenly piped up to say she was going to email Leonora, Umberto lifted his head from the pillow. "Why are you bringing our daughter into this? And exactly why are you doing this?"

"I want to know if he gave her any references."

"No. I mean *exactly why*. Why is Lana's love life so important to you all of a sudden?"

"Because she's like family. *And* she's a valuable asset to us."

Umberto sighed. "This is all too much, Silvana. Can we please go to sleep?"

'Yes, yes. Now that I have a plan, I can sleep."

"Well, I'm glad *you* can because this will probably keep me awake," he muttered grumpily.

"No, no. It's good. It will bring me peace of mind. And if I am at peace, you will be at peace."

He was not convinced of that.

Roger, the long-haired black cat, and Molly, the blue-point Siamese, were tucked in with Ariel and Jimmy, their purring almost vibrating the covers. Jimmy put his book down. "I forgot to tell you that Gordon Greenwood popped into the station today."

"He did? Why didn't you invite him to dinner?"

"Why would I? He and Eileen eat together now. I wouldn't want to stick a fork between them."

She grinned. "No, I guess not. Did he come for a reason?"

"No. Just to say hello. He's rented a house to the director of *Paradise Pines* and just wanted to pass along the information. He said the man was a complete jerk."

"Oh, he must be talking about Berens Nygaard. I think that's the director's name. He's quite famous."

"That's who it is. And he was, a long time ago. Greenwood said he was full of himself and treated him like a country bumpkin."

"So, he's rented a house. That means they'll be here for a while. Where is this house?"

"On the corner of Hyacinth and Larch."

"Oh, my goodness! There's another coincidence. You know that man I met today at Justine's? He lives on Hyacinth."

"Yeah, you mentioned that during dinner."

"I did?"

"Yes."

"Hmm. I don't remember that."

Jimmy patted her arm. "Don't worry, honey. I love you, even though you're getting senile."

She punched him. He ducked away and laughed. The cats looked up, realized they wouldn't have to move, and went back to their pre-sleep purring.

Five

Wednesday, October 22nd

Keith Kittridge, Editor of *The Bayside Bugle,* opened one of the envelopes lying atop the bills in his "Get To" box. The first was a letter for *Brickbats and Bouquets* from Vivian Hoffmeyer, the pinch-mouthed president of the Britannia Bay Horticultural Society. She was going on about the artificial flowers and shrubs stuck in every available receptacle around the tourist centre. Spring bulbs had been planted in all of them and she was sure they would be stabbed by the plastic spikes. She wanted the town compensated by the *Paradise Pines* "outfit" for any damage.

He opened the second envelope and glanced down at the signature. He smiled, then read the message. It was another complaint for the same column, only this one was about cables tripping up seniors. The wording was polite but pointed, and dollars to doughnuts wasn't written by Delilah Moore. Her language would have been saltier. Putting the two letters in the same column on the same day was sure to cause some eyebrows to raise and tongues to wag. This would probably be one of the first times the two old ladies agreed on something. Guessing their reactions, he smirked.

Chief Wyatt had walked over to where the filming was going on and watched for a few minutes as the camera slid down the dolly track following the action. The actors were speaking their lines, but you couldn't hear them over the ambient noise in the plaza and on the street. He wondered how that was going to be dealt with. At least the director hadn't demanded silence in the plaza while they were shooting.

He circled around in front of the art gallery and the fountain honouring a beloved choral director who had died in March, then back up Church Street where he saw J.D. at her post. "How's it going, Constable?" Gawkers stood nearby, and addressing her as J.D would have lessened her authority.

She straightened up and almost saluted, then caught herself. "It's been okay, sir. Everyone has been very cooperative. Probably because there's something to watch."

"Doesn't look all that interesting to me."

She laughed. "Especially after you've seen it a half dozen times."

"I'm wondering how they're going to cut out all the noise."

"I've been getting to know some of the crew and that was one of the first questions I asked. It seems they've taken a page out of how they shoot films in Italy where they let all the noise go on–like you could shut up a bunch of Italians–and afterwards they just remove it and replace it with the sounds they want."

"But what about the actor's lines? You have to hear those."

"The actors go into a room at the studio and watch the scene and say their lines and they slot them in. It's like lip syncing, but they call it looping. By the way, they're wrapping this scene and striking the set tomorrow, so I won't be needed here anymore."

Wyatt started to laugh. "Just listen to you. You'd think you'd grown up in Hollywood."

She grinned. "I've learned a lot of words I'm sure I'll never need."

"Oh, I don't know. My wife does crossword puzzles and she says she's always finding obscure stuff that she filed away in her brain years ago. So if you do them, you might need to know it."

"Hmm. I don't. But maybe that's a good way to pass time. Anyway, if I'm not needed here can I return to my normal duties?"

"Well, that's why I dropped by, J.D. They're going down to a house next to Heritage Gardens on Friday for a couple of days. So they'll need you on Bayside Drive to keep traffic moving."

She sighed. "So, just for a couple of days?"

"That's what I've been told by the mayor. If they drag it out, I'll raise a stink. We're coming up to Hallowe'en and I need all my team for that."

She nodded. "Okay. Thanks."

"Thank *you*," he said, and left.

J.D. heard, "Action!" and returned to her duties, such as they were.

Wyatt felt a slow burn on the way back to the station. Making a decision, he picked up his phone and called the mayor. "Pieter, I'm pulling our constable after tomorrow."

"What? Why?" Verhagen sputtered.

"Because they're finishing up on Church Street. They don't need a nanny watching over unruly citizens."

"But they've asked for traffic control on Bayside Drive."

"Well, they're not going to get it. They don't need it. They're going to have their own security guy posted at the entrance to the property. That's all they need. Traffic might slow down for a look-see, and frankly, the cars need to reduce their speed on Bayside Drive anyway."

Verhagen answered after a long pause. "I suppose you're right. But you don't have to deal with that Benson chap."

"Well, I'd be glad to. If he gives you any guff, just send him my way. You don't have to worry about them pulling out of Britannia Bay and taking their money with them. They're pretty much committed to filming here. I hear they've even rented a house for the director for couple of months."

"Really? Well, then, I won't worry. I'd like nothing better than to send him your way if he decides to give me anymore aggro."

That sorted, Wyatt turned to other matters. He looked into the squad room. Detective Sergeant Ray Rossini and his partner, D.S. Jimmy Tan stood together, talking. Not for the first time, Wyatt was reminded of the nicknames he had silently given them when they were first partnered up–Laurel and Hardy. Rossini was tall, with obvious muscles. His manner was blunt, gruff. Tan's lithe frame held hidden strength, honed though years of training in Asian martial arts. He was subtle, polite. The two men couldn't be more different. Sometimes it worked. Sometimes it didn't. But they got the job done. That's all that mattered to Wyatt.

He called Rossini into his office. "What's going on, Ray? Anything urgent?"

"Nope. It's all quiet."

"I'm pulling Dussault from that assignment. She's too good to waste on crap stuff. Any future traffic detail goes to Paulson."

Ray smiled. "Well, I suppose if you can't fire him, you can make his life as unpleasant as possible."

"Exactly. Okay. That's all," he said, dismissing Ray. He pulled up his personnel files and began reading each one methodically. There had to be a way to upgrade Dussault. Each member of his team seemed exemplary, except for Paulson. He was proud of them. He thought about his list of six attributes that made for a good cop in addition to their basic training. Communication skills; compassion and empathy; integrity; negotiating skills; eagerness to learn; and mental agility. Next, he checked his budget. And winced. Promotion to Constable 2nd class would mean a chunk of money that would be hard to find amongst the line items. He began going through them. Then he had a thought.

Percy Goodbody's fingers were dusted with flour when he heard the sound of a large truck trundling by. Wiping off his hands on a paper towel, he walked to the front window. The truck stopped at the other end of the short street. His curiosity piqued, he stepped outside and watched as a couple of men lifted boxes from the truck. A man came out of the house, said something, and they followed him into the house. Percy figured he was from the film company.

Curiosity satisfied, he went back to his baking. He had promised Ida at Off Yer Rockers that he would bake an apple pie for her customers. With all the apples he had picked at Jade's, he decided to make one more for himself. And he would still have enough fruit left over for the candy apples he was planning to make for Hallowe'en. Kids loved them, especially because they were something special and home-made; not something they could get any day of the week from a store.

Humming to himself, he recalled the day spent with Jade Errington. He always enjoyed his time with her. To the town, she might be the resident hippie, but to him, she was a link to the past and to the memory of his daughter. *God rest her soul.*

Six

Tamsyn Foxcroft had a moment's panic when Chief Wyatt called her in to his office. She ran through some recent events and wondered if someone had lodged a complaint against her, but came up with nothing. But then again, what was a slight to some white person when compared to the invectives thrown her way over the years?

Gesturing, Wyatt told Tamsyn to close the door and take a chair. "I've got a situation here. I'm wondering if you can help me with it."

To Tamsyn, this sounded like soft-soaping administration speak. It surprised her because Wyatt was usually straightforward.

"I'm thinking of promoting J.D. But I want your input first."

Tamsyn did her best to hide the relief on her face.

Wyatt chuckled. "You thought you were going to get a dressing down, eh?"

She smiled sheepishly and shrugged.

"I'm also asking Mary Beth to give me her two cents' worth."

"This sounds interesting, boss. What do you want me to do?"

"I know you don't have much opportunity to work with J.D., but what are your impressions of her so far? And I don't want the cop stuff. I want the personality stuff that makes for a better cop." He pulled out his list of six items and read them out.

As Tamsyn listened, she wondered about her own personal attributes. Did they match those on the list? "Hmm. Let me think for a sec." She settled back in her chair. After a few moments, she asked him for the first item, then gave him her opinion. She repeated the request for each item, and followed up.

Wyatt was impressed. "Well, Tamsyn, I have to say, you certainly have communication skills."

"Thanks, boss. That's nice to hear."

"Now, not a word to anyone. It may not happen and I wouldn't want her to be set up for a fall."

"Got it."

"Okay. That's all."

Tamsyn went to her desk and wrote down the list of six characteristics, and then stuck it in her vest pocket. She planned to do some serious research–on herself.

After she left, Wyatt picked up the budget sheet and walked to the photocopy machine. He took a copy to Mary Beth, one of the personnel who worked the phones and front counter. Stepping inside her cubicle he crouched down beside her, his knees cracking as he did so.

"Oh, boy. I hope that isn't as painful as it sounds," she said.

"It only hurts when I get up," he said. He handed her the budget sheet. "I've got some homework for you."

"What's this?"

"It's the operating budget. I want you to go through it line-by-line and try to find some things we can cut. I've looked at it so many times over the years that I can't see past the obvious anymore."

"How much are you looking at trimming?"

"About twenty-four hundred per annum."

"Yikes! Maybe you should look at the capital budget, Chief."

'I may have to do that, too. But let's start here. There must be little things we order more than we need, like boxes of paper clips and toner and pencils and paper. Even toilet paper and soap."

"Okay. I get your drift. How much time do you need?"

"It's not urgent. I just want you to be as thorough as possible. You worked for an accountant once."

"It was a lot easier than fielding complaints as a customer service clerk, I can tell you."

"Then why did you quit?"

"The guy had busy hands, and in those days it was his word against mine."

"It still is, a lot of the time."

"You got that right. I'll get on this tonight."

"Thanks, Mary Beth. You're a mensch." As he rose, his knees cracked. She winced.

Seven

Thursday, October 23rd

F or heaven's sake, Sara. Stop dancing. How do you expect me to get
these wings aligned when you're jumping all over the place?"

Sara stopped. "What does 'aligned' mean?"

"It means having them the same on both sides. Now lift your arms
while I adjust these ribbons."

For a few moments the house and its inhabitants remained still as
Annika concentrated on the task at hand. Satisfied, she squatted and
looked Sara in the eye. "Now, Fairy Princess. Do you want to see what
they will look like on Hallowe'en?"

"Yes!" She ran over to the three-way-mirror. "Oh, Mommy. They
are so beautiful! I wish I could wear them forever."

"I'll get lots of pictures of you, and I'll take my camera to the
Community Centre. And maybe a photographer will see fit to get your
picture in *The Bayside Bugle*. Now, let's get them off you and get ready
to go to Ariel's."

"Can I wear them to Ariel's?"

"No, certainly not. They're too fragile."

"What does 'fragile' mean?"

"It means they're easy to break. Now lift your arms again so that I
can untie the ribbons."

That done, they got ready to leave. Maisie, sensing that they were
leaving, got up from her bed and looked at them expectantly. "I would
love to take you, Maisie, but Ariel has *cats*, and I don't think you

would be welcome." The little beagle seemed to understand what "cats" meant, and slunk back to her bed.

Ariel was at the piano playing and singing when the doorbell rang. She jumped. She had been so immersed in the beauty of the melody, that the metallic sound seemed to come from some other universe. Answering, she saw Annika and Sara. Of course. She had invited them over to discuss the idea of asking Jade Errington for help with bee information.

"Hi, Ariel. We could hear your singing. It was beautiful," Annika said.

"Thank you. Come on in."

"The song was in German, wasn't it?"

"Yes. It's Schubert. It's called *Du bist die Ruh.*"

"What does it mean?" Sara asked.

"It's about rest and peace. Now, come into the kitchen, Let's have tea and cookies and see how we're going to approach Jade."

Ariel opened a tin of loose-leaf tea, and immediately Sara blurted out, "Oh. That's Earl Grey. It's Mommy's favourite."

Ariel glanced at her friend, a question in her eyes.

"She can smell things a mile away," Annika explained.

Delilah was fit to be tied. "Do you know what he's done, Melvin?" she asked her deceased husband. "Well, of course you do. You see it all from up there, don't you? Couldn't you have done something? No, I suppose not. You don't interfere with worldly things anymore." She slapped the page of *The Bayside Bugle* with her magnifying glass, jarring Tabitha from her snoozing. "That's what he's done!"

On his way to Off Yer Rockers with his apple pie, Percy heard an argument beside one of the large trailers with the words *Paradise Pines* painted on the side. A man's back was toward him. He had a grip on a woman's arm. She was facing Percy, who caught the defiance in her eyes.

"Just remember who you're dealing with here," the man hissed. "Anymore of that diva shit and *you'll* be written out. You're not the script writer, dearie. You're just an *actress*. Not a star. And if you're not careful, you never will be."

She snatched her arm away, opened the door to the trailer, and slammed it behind her.

Percy snickered. Guess things aren't so peaceful in *Paradise Pines*, he thought.

At Off Yer Rockers, Ida looked up when the door opened. She broke into a smile. "I hope that's my pie, Percy."

"It is. May still be warm. I wrapped it up good." He handed her the cloth bag. "Don't tip it. It's juicy."

"I'll treat it with kid gloves." She took out the pie and smelled it. "Mmm. Cinnamon. This is going to be delicious."

"Course it is." He removed his coat and bush hat then took his regular seat. "So, you're my partner today, eh, Hap?"

"Yep. I drew the short straw." After a few guffaws, the men settled down to their games.

"Did you see today's *Bugle*?" someone asked. "A couple of funny comments in the *Brickbats and Bouquets* column."

"Oh yeah, I read them. I'll bet those two old ladies are hoppin' mad," someone else replied. Then they all discussed what had been said. A few more minutes of silence.

"Does anyone want apple pie?" Ida asked. "Percy just baked it and it smells wonderful."

"You got any ice cream?"

"Ice cream and whipped cream."

"Well, put on a fresh pot of coffee and I'll have a piece."

"Count me in."

"Me too."

"How about you, Percy?" Ida asked. "You going to treat yourself?"

"No, thanks. I have another pie at home."

"Good thing you walk a lot."

"Walking is good for you. And you'd be surprised what you see and hear along the way. I just heard an argument beside one of the film company rigs between some important guy and an actress. He was giving her what for."

As the men tucked into their pies and coffee, Ida took out the copy of the *Bugle*. "I wonder if it was that guy who's been throwing his weight around," she said. "I think his name was mentioned in an article today." It didn't take her long to find the page. "Here it is. Yada, yada, yada … okay. 'The producer, Allen Benson, has been pleased with the cooperation he has received from the townspeople, and especially the Mayor and Police Chief'," she read.

"I hear they brought in a washed-up director who used to be famous," Hap said. "Some Norwegian hot shot who got caught with drugs."

"I heard it was because he got caught with some woman who was a girlfriend of a Mafia boss."

"Whatever. He was sunk."

"He used to be a big fish, now he's just a tadpole," another man said.

As the men chuckled, Ida read farther down the article. "Here's his name. It's Berens Nygaard."

"Guess we'll have to watch our stashes and our women."

Everyone but Percy laughed. Had he heard correctly? His mouth went dry. His pulse sped up. People were talking, but their voices ricocheted around an echo chamber in his eardrums. He stood. He felt strange, like the floor was tilting under his feet. "I think I'll push off," he mumbled. He didn't know where the words came from or how they sounded.

Everyone stared at his ashen face. "You okay, Percy?" Hap asked. "You look like you've seen a ghost."

"Think I just need to get some air."

"It's started to rain. Let me give you a ride."

"No. No. It's just a couple a blocks. And I got my hat."

"My car's right outside," Hap continued, encouragingly.

"It's all right, Hap. Really. I'm okay now." He took a big breath. Some colour had returned to his face. His friends' faces, however, reflected their concern as they watched him leave the premises.

Ida picked up the paper and reread the article. What was in it that had brought on that reaction? She came up empty. Maybe he did just suddenly feel a bit off.

Percy didn't remember covering the short distance. He didn't feel the rain. He didn't feel his feet. He didn't feel his tears. He was in another space. Another time. And it was all bad.

Eight

Friday, October 24th

Umberto and Silvana sat with Ray at his kitchen table. Dinner plates containing a memory of the mushroom and prosciutto lasagne hadn't yet been cleared away. One bottle of wine had been polished off and they were working on a second. It was closing on midnight.

Silvana poured herself a bit more Brunello di Montalcino before making her announcement. "Josefina called me today. I–"

"Your sister *phoned* you?" Umberto broke in.

The look Silvana gave her husband had Ray wanting to hold on to his "jewels."

"Yes, she *phoned* me. I know you think she's the cheapest person in the world."

"I dunno. I think Mayor Verhagen could give her a run for her money," Ray uttered.

"She didn't reverse the charges, did she?" Umberto asked, horrified.

"No, of course not. Anyway, I don't think you can do that internationally. Now, can I proceed, or do you have more questions?"

"Yes. Why did she phone you?"

"Because Leonora told her about my email … my questions about Stefano. Josefina suggested hiring a private detective."

Umberto threw up a hand. "A private investigator? Silvana, you are going too far with this madness."

"It's not madness, Umberto. It's being prudent. She knows of a good one–a man with good credentials. She suggested he start right away."

"And I suppose you agreed," he said, looking as if he had bitten into something sour.

"Yes. She sent me his contact information and I emailed him right away."

He sighed. "I can just imagine how he's going to soak us. He'll pad his expenses, eat at the best restaurants, stay at the best hotels, and drag everything out until he has charged up at least five thousand dollars."

"It so happens that he lives in Torino, so he doesn't have to do that. We are paying a per diem of one hundred dollars. I gave him five days to find out everything and write up a report."

"Why are you doing this again?" Ray asked.

"I am protecting Lana," Silvana said archly.

"Lana's a big girl, Mamma. I'm sure she's been around the block when it comes to men. We don't need to protect her," Ray said.

Umberto tapped the side of his nose. "She may have been around the block but she's most likely not ridden with a real Italian man."

"Yes, that's an Italian experience most women would be wise to avoid. You, and I don't mean you, Umberto, but you Italian men can swear on Madonna that you are telling the truth while lying through your teeth."

"At least we don't swear on our mother's graves," Ray said.

"Now *that* would be blasphemous," Umberto retorted.

Shortly before midnight, Ariel returned to the bedroom from the bathroom. She knew she shouldn't have had coffee after dinner. What was she thinking? Obviously, she wasn't thinking at all. Lately her thoughts were all over the map. Was it that phone call from her brother about her father? He said it wasn't serious. So why did he call her to reassure her? And why should she care?

Rain was beating a percussive symphony on the windows. She moved a shutter and looked at the sheets of it falling in front of the street lamp. About to return to bed, she saw a figure walking up the street hunched over, with only a peaked cap for protection. Who could that be at this time of night? And without a car? A few minutes later, Lana's front porch light came on, but Ariel wouldn't have been able to see that. She was already snuggled next to Jimmy, who hadn't moved. Only the cats were awake.

At three o'clock in the morning, Percy woke up hungry. He warmed up a piece of the apple pie and made a pot of tea. Sitting at the table, he went over what he had learned at Off Yer Rockers. Where was his copy of the *Bugle*? Finding it, he opened it to the offending page. Searching, he saw it. The name he hated above all others. Berens Nygaard. The man who had lured his daughter to Hollywood.

It had taken years to deal with the shock and pain. And the infamy. The love and support from his friends and family had kept him going after he questioned his own existence. His beloved Jeannie had died. Then Blythe was gone. Murdered. He had spent those years on his boat, living in rhythm with the sea and the life of a fisherman. It had sustained him–the mindless hard work softened by the beauty of his surroundings. He believed Mother Nature had eventually healed him.

But now that man had entered his world, opening old wounds. It wouldn't do. Wouldn't do at all. Something had to be done about it.

Nine

Sunday, October 26th

It's too bad you won't be able to see the bees, Sara," Ariel said. "But Jade said she has little chicks."

"Oh. They're so cute. Then they grow up and turn ugly. It's backwards. They should be like the ugly duckling who grows up to be a beautiful swan."

Annika smiled. "That's right. So you're not too disappointed?"

"Well … maybe a little bit."

"I'm sure you'll see lots more than chicks," Ariel assured her. But she and Annika wouldn't be able to see much of anything. Jade had made it clear that the tour was for Sara only. She loved children, but barely tolerated adults.

When they pulled up to Jade's fenced-in property, Sara stuck her nose out the window and reported that she smelled lavender. She was right. Stacks of dried blossoms were heaped on large sacks. After Jade opened the gate, Sara jumped out of the car, but then stood shyly by as Ariel made the introductions. When Jade smiled at Sara, the aforementioned protruding teeth stood out like sentinels. Sara had been warned not to stare or say anything.

Jade leaned down so that her eyes met Sara's. "I'm glad you came even though the bees are asleep until the spring. But I can show you the chicks, if you like."

"Oh, yes! Please."

Winding their way between a two-storey wood shingle house and a large greenhouse they saw several chickens eating greens and pecking at the ground for whatever else they could find. A few were inside the large open-air chicken run attached to the coop. "Let's go inside," Jade said.

The first thing that surprised Sara was the pleasant aroma. She was expecting worse. "I like that smell," Sara said.

"What does it smell like?"

"Like a forest."

"Those are the pine chips that cover the floor."

"It's warm in here."

"Yes, chickens need to keep warm and have light or they won't lay eggs."

Several rows of nesting boxes lined two sides of the coop. "Here are the hens," Jade said.

"How come the boxes are so high off the ground?"

"They're called nesting boxes. Chickens feel safer when they're off the ground. Their only defence is to fly away, and chickens aren't the world's greatest aviators."

Sara peeked into the boxes filled with straw and wood shavings. "The chickens look so cozy. You can hardly see them." Then she saw names on most of the boxes. "How come you name them?"

"I think of them as little girls, so they have to have names."

Sara nodded as though that made perfect sense. "What are these little boxes underneath for?"

"Those are their toilets."

Sara started to giggle.

"Chickens poop, even when they're asleep. So these little trays underneath help to make my job easier because these nesting boxes have to be cleaned every day."

"How come the food and water trays are hanging up?"

"That's to make sure no poop gets in them."

"How come there are bells hanging on strings?"

"Believe it or not, chickens get bored. So these are toys."

"Really?"

"That's right."

"Where are the chicks?"

"They're in the brooder." Jade opened another section of the coop. "This is where I keep the babies."

"Oh!" Sara exclaimed when she saw six tiny chicks in an open-topped box. "Oh, they're so cute. Can I pick one up?"

"I'm afraid not, Sara. They're still very fragile."

"I just learned that word. It means they could break."

"Yes. Their little legs are easily broken or sprained."

Sara pointed to the strange contraption above the box. "What's this?"

"It's called an electric hen. See how they gather under it to keep warm?"

"Do you know which hen is their mother?"

"I do. C'mon and I'll show you."

Back in the coop, Jade pointed out a nesting box with the word "Sheila" painted on it. "She's their mother. A couple of hens don't have names yet. Would you like one to have your name?"

Sara clapped her hands together. "I would love that!"

They went out into the chicken run, and Jade pointed out three hens. Sara chose a Plymouth Rock. "I've never seen a black and white chicken before. You have lots of different chickens."

"Before you leave today, I'll give you some eggs that Sara laid this morning."

Sara laughed. "That sounds so funny."

When they finally emerged, Sara ran up to her mother. "I have a chicken named after me and we're bringing home eggs that she laid this morning."

Passing the greenhouse, Sara asked what was inside. When Jade said, "special plants," Ariel was hoping she didn't mean marijuana. Jade opened the door. Sara frowned and stepped back. "What's that awful smell?"

"Sara!" Annika admonished her. "Don't be rude."

Jade laughed. "She's not being rude. She's being honest. It's the smell of patchouli. Some people don't like it. Others do. I'm making oil out of the plants. Let's get out of here and go to the house."

Inside, the smell of lavender once again permeated the air.

"I love the smell of lavender, though," Sara said, trying to make up for her rash comment.

"Just a second." Jade left the room then returned with several lavender sachets tied with tiny satin ribbons. "These will be nice in your dresser drawers." She gave two to Sara and one each to Annika and Ariel. "And because you couldn't see the bees today, I'll give you some of their honey." Reaching into a cupboard, she brought out three jars filled with the amber fluid.

"Oh, this is a real treasure," Ariel said.

"Thank you for everything, Jade," Annika said. "It's been a lovely visit."

"And you've been a lovely visitor," she said to Sara. "I'm looking forward to the spring when you come back and see the bees."

"Oh, me too! Thank you very much."

On the way home, Sara told them that she really, really didn't like the smell of patchouli, and they broke out in laughter.

When the visitors left, Jade gave a great sigh and sat at her kitchen table. It was too much outside stimulation for one day. Her phone chirped. It was Percy, and the news caused a further cleft in the day. Berens Nygaard was in town directing a TV show. Didn't he know he was not safe here?

Ten

Delilah had eaten too many dessert squares at church. But the compliments about her complaint in *The Bayside Bugle* had kept the conversation going and she couldn't just sit there and do nothing. She agreed with someone who said that Kittridge should have waited and put in Vivian's submission on another day. It seemed a mean-spirited thing to do. When someone else said that it was nice to see the two women agree on something, Delilah decided it was time to leave. She was a Christian, but not *that* Christian! What she needed now was a proper lunch.

She was reaching for crackers and a can of cream of tomato soup when the doorbell rang. Tabitha, sleeping on the sofa, hightailed it to the bedroom. *Sunday afternoon? I hope it's not more of those JWs. I thought I got rid of them once and for all.* Standing on the stoop, smiling, were Ariel, Annika and Sara.

"Hello, there." She bent down. "And a special hello to you, Sara. I haven't seen you for a while."

"I brought you a present," she said excitedly, holding out a jar of honey.

"Well, aren't you sweet? Just like this honey. Come on in."

"And here's a lavender sachet for your drawers."

"Oh, isn't this pretty. I can guess where you've been this morning."

"Jade showed me her chicks and I got a hen named after me. We have eggs that she laid this morning."

Delilah laughed. "Well, mercy me. That must have been fun."

"And in the spring I'm going back to see the bees when they wake up."

While Delilah put away the honey, Ariel spotted a photograph on the mantel. Returning to the living room, Delilah saw Ariel quickly shift her eyes away from it. "I took it out of the trunk," she said. "I can finally look at him without crying."

Sara, sensing the old woman's sudden sadness, slipped her hand inside Delilah's gnarled fingers. Delilah smiled softly. "You're just a wonderful little girl. You know that?"

After they left, Sara asked Ariel about the picture.

"That was her son, Scott. He died in a plane crash many years ago."

"Oh, that's sad. I'm glad I gave her the honey and lavender."

Jimmy was vigorously polishing all his shoes when Ariel walked in. It was well past lunchtime and her stomach was grumbling.

"How was your visit at Jade's?"

"Really interesting," she said absently, reaching into the fridge, pulling out leftovers, and placing a bowl of noodles in clam sauce in the microwave.

"Just interesting?" he said, finishing off a pair of leather loafers.

"Well, I learned a few things about chickens." Ariel got out the utensils, salt and pepper, and a napkin, and put them on the table. "But she wouldn't let us ask any questions. Just Sara." She opened the fridge again. "I was sure I put an opened bottle of white wine in here." Pushing things this way and that and not finding it, she closed the door. "When did I drink that wine? I don't remember drinking it."

"Well, don't look at me."

"I'm losing it." The microwave beeped. Steam rose from the dish. She took the bowl to the table and blew on the hot food. "One funny thing, though. We went into the greenhouse where she was growing patchouli plants. She makes oil. Sara wrinkled up her nose and said 'What's that smell?' Well, it does stink. Sort of like dirty socks." She began eating and that was the end of that conversation.

Jimmy put away his shoes. "Do you want to go for a walk?"

"I'm up for that. It's quite nice out."

During the walk she told him about seeing Scott Moore's picture on Delilah's mantel. "She said she can finally look at him without crying."

"There's nothing worse for parents than losing a child."

"I wonder if it will be as bad when we lose Roger and Molly."

"When Mr. Bojangles' dog up and died, after twenty years he still grieved."

Ariel laughed. "You're nuts, do you know that?"

"But remember, a pet is not your own flesh and blood. So it can't be as heartbreaking. Some parents never recover."

"Speaking of parents. I got a call from Jeffrey. He said my father had fallen. They put it down to a stroke. But that it wasn't serious. So why did he call me, then? And why should I care, anyway? He's been an absolute bastard all these years."

"He's still your father, don't forget."

"Would you have been as magnanimous about *your* father?"

He winced. "Touché"

"We're both the children of terrible fathers."

"At least you had a relationship with him before I came along."

"Then he showed his true colors. He was despicable. Never saying he was sorry for what he called you."

"Never mind, honey. I've been called worse than 'goddamn Chink'."

"I often wondered if he had said it to your face if you would have punched him in the nose."

"I'm a peace officer, Ariel. I wouldn't have done that." He took a couple of steps. "Maybe a Muay Thai kick to the back of his knee."

She laughed out loud. "I would loved to have seen that."

He clasped her hand. "Seriously, Ariel, have you thought about what you will do when he dies?"

"Many times."

"And?"

"I change my mind so often that I don't know." She fell silent.

They continued their walk in the same vein.

Eleven

Wednesday, October 29th

At Off Yer Rockers, the men were multi-tasking, concentrating on their cribbage games while noshing and gossiping. "Did you hear about the gillnetter that lost its power in Broughton Strait?"

"That was Vern Cruickshank."

"Yeah. Crankshaft. Never keeps his boat in decent running shape. Probably his fuel filter. Sees how long he can go without replacing it. His electricals needed upgrading years ago, but he's too cheap and too lazy. He's damn lucky Perchie was nearby. Towed him to Sointula."

"If it'd been me I'd've just left him on his own. Maybe then he'd learn his lesson."

"You can't do that, Arnie. You're not a fisherman. You don't understand. It's the law of the sea."

"I'll bet Perchie was pissed off. Missed an opening."

"Lost time *and* money."

Ida, busy clearing away lunch dishes from another table, interrupted them. "Anyone know where Percy is? Hasn't shown his face around here in two days."

"I was thinking about that myself," Hap said. "Maybe I should call him." He got out his cellphone. "Hi Percy. We were just wondering where you've been keeping yourself ... Oh, is that right? Well, I won't keep you then. See you when we see you."

"Is he okay?" Ida asked.

"He's fine. He's busy making candy apples for the kids for Hallowe'en."

"Percy's a prince."

"Someone's reporting fireworks going off," Mary Beth said, swiveling around in her chair, addressing everyone and holding out a post-it note.

Ray pointed to Simon Verdun-Jones. "You take that, Simon."

The little Welshman pulled a face as he got up and retrieved the slip of paper. "This is out in the Township," he said sourly. "And it'll be a wild goose chase." What it might do was make him late for his tea. Glynis would not be pleased.

As if reading his mind, Ray ribbed him as he made his way out the exit. "What's the problem, Simon? You'll be back in time to get home for dinner."

A couple of the officers threw dirty looks at Ray. Wives were a touchy subject on the squad and they sympathized with Simon. So far everyone had dodged the bullet. No divorces … a rarity within the peace-keeping community.

Simon returned, sooner than expected. "Surprise. Surprise. The culprits had already done a runner," he said with disgust. He dropped a half dozen rockets on his desk just as Tamsyn arrived. "I found these, though."

"Look familiar, Foxcroft?" Ray asked, pointedly.

She glanced at the rockets, then at Ray, then back at the rockets. She had an idea who was selling this particular rocket, but her unreadable face gave away nothing. It was none of her business if a female elder wanted to bring in some extra cash. "Nope," she said, blandly.

Like hell, Ray thought. But he wasn't going to step into that minefield. He and Tamsyn had come to some kind of truce two years before and so far it remained intact. No sense upsetting the applecart.

Delilah opened the box of seventy individually wrapped packages of fruit gummies. She worried. Last year she had run out, but two boxes would be too many. She decided to get some back-ups at Bayside Foods and have a chat with Barb, her favourite cashier. Struggling into her jacket and getting her walker, she looked for her cat. "Going shopping, Tabitha!" she shouted when she couldn't find her. *Probably under the duvet.*

When she arrived at the plaza, she was glad to see no indication that a television crew had once crowded out every bit of space in and around the area. Inside the store, she eyed all the candy on display. Her sweet tooth began kicking in. She loved chocolate. If she had leftovers, she would make sure they had chocolate in them. She spied a box of Lindt chocolate balls filled with assorted flavors. *Oh, perfect!*

At the checkout, Barb looked at her slyly. "These are your just-in-cascrs, ch? Glad to see you picked something healthy," she said, poking fun at her.

"I've got healthy things–fruit gummies. The kids will get a lot of those. Nobody hands out chocolate anymore–well, except for peanut butter cups. They'll love these. And if I have any leftovers, then I want something I like."

"You won't get any argument from me about that."

Delilah rushed home. Now, if she could just eat only one, she would be okay. But there was something about chocolate …

Stefano Moretti didn't understand. "You hand out food on Hallowe'en night to kids?"

Georgina chuckled. "Not food, Stefano. Just little treats. They come every year and we always give them something. So this year Lana is baking miniature Italian meatball cookies."

"Wow! All that sugar and chocolate! The kids will be bouncing off the ceiling."

"That's the point."

"What … to make the lives of parents even crazier?"

"Parents get to have fun, too, you know. It's something to do until Christmas arrives."

"Followed by Easter."

"Oh, no. Valentine's Day comes next."

"So many holidays."

"You have to have diversions, Stefano. You know, some chocolate with the bread. You have holidays in Italy."

"But most of our holidays are religious."

"So, a little wine with your bread."

Silvana had listened to the conversation with more than passing interest. The report from the detective in Torino had arrived. That evening she shared it with Umberto. After carefully reading it, they sat back with wonder on their faces.

"So what is he doing working in restaurants? For that matter, why does he even bother working?" Silvana asked.

"Maybe he loves cooking. It's an avocation, not a necessity," Umberto said. "We both used to love it, remember? We would get all excited about a recipe. It was a creative thing for us. Maybe it's the same for him. He can quit anytime, obviously. Besides, one needs a good reason to get up in the morning. You can't be a lay-about if you want to have some self-respect."

"Well, I won't worry about Lana now if she decides to take up with the man," Silvana said. "But why the secrets, I wonder?"

"If you fell in love with someone, wouldn't you want to keep your fortune a mystery at first? By the way, maybe it's time I told you about those gold bars I have stashed in a secret vault."

Silvana rolled up the report and swatted him.

Twelve

Hallowe'en night

Goodbody had been handing out his candy apples wrapped in waxed paper while anxiously keeping an eye out for the fairy princess. It was getting close to the start of festivities at the Community Centre. That meant probably no more children would be trick or treating. He put out a small table and tray with the last of the apples. It was unfortunate that he missed her. But he couldn't wait any longer. He had to get ready.

Berens Nygaard had purchased lights and animatronics worthy of *The Nightmare before Christmas,* and roped in some crew members to help set up the display. He hoped it would earn him some cred with the locals, and by all accounts it was working. For several days, as soon as it got dark, people arrived to take in the spine-chilling scene and eerie sounds.

Now he, the Weapons Master and Script Supervisor were going through the dailies to see if they could splice anything together from today's botched scene. They scrolled through the film until they reached the segment with the misfiring gun. The sound of kids arriving interrupted them. Even though they had serious matters to sort out, they took the time to pass out treats and ooh and aah over the costumes, no matter how tacky they were.

After deciding how to proceed with the scene the next day, Nygaard sent them on their way. That done, he defrosted a pizza. Putting out two paper plates, he cut one slice, left the rest on the table and returned to reviewing the rushes and handing out goodies. His visitor wouldn't be arriving until much later.

Closing in on six o'clock, a little girl dressed as a fairy came by, eyes filled with wonder. He was struck by how angelic she looked, contrasting that with the witch who was standing behind her. He thought it was the girl's mother, then saw another adult at curbside. As the little girl thanked him and ran back to the road, the witch spoke up in a scratchy voice. "I have a trick for you."

"You do?" Nygaard laughed. A sudden blow to his chest sent him reeling back into the room and crashing to the floor. His elbows took the brunt of the fall and pain seared through his arms. "What the hell?" He struggled to get up from his vulnerable position. "What do you want? I don't have much cash, but you're welcome to it."

"I don't want your dirty money! I want you to get out of town!"

When he saw that the witch wasn't holding a weapon, Nygaard's initial fright subsided. He got himself up off the floor. "Who the hell are you?" Just as he was sizing up whether he could tackle the person, the witch removed his hat and mask and flung them at Nygaard's feet.

"You don't know who I am, do you?" he asked.

Nygaard stared into the face of an old man. An angry old man with a purpose. Always dangerous. He had to placate him somehow. "No. I'm sorry. I don't. Should I?"

"Does the name Blythe O'Neill mean anything to you?"

Jesus! Blythe. A name that haunted him still.

"Well, I'm her father."

Her father? What the hell is he doing here?

"And you've come to this town where she was born and raised … and buried. Your presence here is staining her memory. I want you out of Britannia Bay. Go back to Hollywood."

"Blythe was from Britannia Bay? That's news to me. I thought she was from Vancouver. At least, that's what I was led to believe." He searched his memory. Yes, that's what she had told him.

"She wouldn't have wanted anyone to know she was just a small-town girl."

"You'd be surprised at the number of stars who come from small towns, Mr. O'Neill."

"That's not my name. And that wasn't her name, either. It was Goodbody. Can you imagine the jokes if she had used that name? That's why she changed it."

Nygaard recalled his first meeting with Blythe and agreed with what the old man was saying. Jokes about her breasts—or rack, as they were crudely called—would have been endless.

"She wanted to be a bona fide actress," Goodbody continued. "She even took acting lessons and hired a coach." He paused. "In many ways, she was like Marilyn Monroe."

Nygaard noticed that the original fire in the man's manner was ebbing. He hoped to reason with him and get him out of the house.

"What is it you want?" That was his first mistake. The man's ire returned.

"I told you. I want you out of Britannia Bay! Go back to Hollywood where you belong."

"I can't do that, Mr. Goodbody. This show has become a hit and revived my career. I can't give that up."

"But Blythe gave up her life!"

"That had nothing to do with me!" His second mistake.

"Oh, didn't it? You used her then passed her on to someone else who killed her ... and defiled her corpse."

"She used me, too. It was a fair trade." Another mistake.

"Fair trade? You think sleeping with a naïve young woman is a fair trade for the bit parts you doled out?"

"It's part of Hollywood, Mr. Goodbody. The girls all know that. That's why it's called a casting couch. There's hardly a woman you see on the screen who hasn't slept for the part. Only the very talented with genuine acting experience can make it without spreading their legs." His final mistake.

In a rage, Goodbody lunged at him. Nygaard's foot caught on the witch hat. He fell, hitting his head on the edge of the coffee table. He groaned. His body went slack. He lay still.

Goodbody, still wearing the costume's long black gloves, checked for a pulse. He couldn't find one. *Oh, my God!* His mind racing, he thought of only one thing. Getting out of there. He picked up his hat and mask and flew out the back door.

Sara and her mother arrived home from the Community Centre, high on excitement. Maisie, caught up in the mood, danced around their feet. "Do you think my picture will be in the paper, Mommy?"

"Of course it will, sweetie. All the winners' pictures will be in the paper."

Sara dumped her stash of goodies on the table. As she removed the candy apple, she sighed. "I wish Mr. Goodbody had been at home. I wanted him to see my fairy wings."

"Maybe he was somewhere else when you came by, and you missed him."

"How come he left candy apples outside?"

"Maybe he just decided to leave them for anyone who came by. But he'll see your picture in the paper. And we have all the pictures on the cellphone that we sent Daddy. Maybe we'll see Mr. Goodbody again and we can show them to him."

"It's not the same thing." She complained.

"No. A picture may be worth a thousand words, but it can't capture every facet of a moment."

"I think I know what you mean."

"Good. Now, do you think you can get yourself ready for bed? I have to take Maisie for a short walk."

The dog immediately pulled the leash down from the hanger and hung it in her mouth.

Sara hugged her. "You're such a good doggie."

Annika took the key, let herself and Maisie out, locked the door, then waited while Maisie immediately relieved herself on an azalea bush. "I hate to say this, Maisie, but sometimes you're not such a good girl."

Jimmy and Ariel were sitting on a log drinking cocoa and watching the people dancing near the bonfire.

"That's a pretty decent band," Jimmy said.

"I love real rock music."

Jimmy noticed her head bopping. "Wanna dance?"

"I thought you'd never ask!" Laughing, they got up and found space within the growing throng.

After a few tunes, the band stopped. "Ladies and gentlemen. The fireworks are about to start. So that's it for us for tonight. But we're gonna be at the Chai 'n Chill Pub tomorrow night and next weekend. So come on by and enjoy the food and special ales and, need I say, the great music."

"Do you want to stay for the fireworks?" Ariel asked.

"Nah. It's getting cold and I'm getting too long in the tooth for these late nights." He yawned. "Let's go home. Thank God tomorrow is day off."

As they were getting ready for bed, they talked about the costume contest at the Community Centre, and agreed that Sara's deserved first prize in her category.

"I like the ones that parents make or the kids make themselves," Ariel said. "Too many are store bought, like those robots. I didn't see any ghosts this year."

"No. That's too easy. And no witches either."

Percy stood over an old wash tub from his former fishing boat, stripping the costume into shreds and covering them with a solution of vinegar and hot water. Blythe had worn the costume as a teenager and it still reeked of the patchouli that she and Jade regularly doused on themselves. His heart ached as he destroyed something that had belonged to her, but he knew he had been seen by the mother of the fairy princess. She had been waiting at the end of Nygaard's long front sidewalk. But did she see him enter? That, he didn't know. And what about those boys who were not far behind her? Did they see him? He had no choice and carried on with his task, full of fear … and tears.

Thirteen

Saturday, November 1st

An agitated driver from *Paradise Pines* pounded on Nygaard's door. He checked his watch again. Nygaard had said to pick him up at seven o'clock. It was already seven-fifteen. The house was dark. The fierce-looking inflatables that had been full of air just hours before were flaccid and eerily quiet. It gave him the creeps. He continued banging on the door.

"What's all this racket?" a male voice hollered.

The driver turned and saw a flashlight beam coming up the sidewalk. "I'm trying to wake up Mr. Nygaard." He made a fist as though to carry on with his hammerings.

"Stop!" the man ordered. "I have a key."

He has a key? Does Nygaard know this? He'll probably shit a brick when he finds out. Or maybe he's a security guard.

The man gently nudged him aside and inserted the key into the lock. Feeling no resistance in the tumbler, he realized the door was unlocked. Something didn't seem right. He cracked open the door. The stench hit him. He pulled his head back.

The driver began to push him aside.

"Stop! You can't go in."

"What do you mean, I can't go in? Why not?"

"I smell something." He took out his ever-present handkerchief and held it across his face.

"What is it, gas?"

"Just stay where you are." Leaving the puzzled driver outside, he stepped inside, closing and locking the door. He flipped the light switch. No power. His flashlight beam picked up what he was afraid he would find—Berens Nygaard splayed on his back with his guts spilling onto the floor. Using his handkerchief, he picked up a phone by the sofa and dialed 9-1-1. "I'd like to report what appears to be a homicide." The dispatcher, took down the details and said she would get right on it.

He found the breaker. Seconds later, a few indoor lamps and all the outdoor lights illuminated. A moment after that, the ghoulish outdoor display died a quick death. He opened the door and did his best to prevent the driver from peering inside, but he ducked his head under the man's arm for a quick peek.

Colour drained from his face. "Is that a body? Is it Mr. Nygaard?"

The man pushed him back and shut the door. "Yes. It's Mr. Nygaard and he is deceased." His tone was brusque. "And it could very well be a homicide."

"A homicide? How do you know that? Are you a cop or something?"

"No, I'm the town undertaker."

Georgina was already up preparing coffee when she heard Ray's cellphone. At this hour, she figured it meant trouble. And he wasn't answering. He had had several glasses of wine and a heavy meal the night before, putting him into a state worthy of Hypnos. She ran into the bedroom and picked up the phone while prodding her husband. "Hi, Chief Wyatt. It's Georgina. I'm trying to raise the lummox."

Ray snapped awake. He grabbed the phone. "What's up, Chief?" He listened. "Where? … We'll be there as soon as I get my pants … Who? Well, hot damn! This town is finally going to be on the map."

Jimmy was dressed, bolting down a bagel as he waited for Ray to pick him up. Ariel, dumbfounded, attempted to eat her muesli. "Wyatt said it was murder?"

"Apparently Quentin Pickell called 9-1-1. And he would know."

"Kewpie? How come he was there?"

"He lives next door, and if I know Gordon Greenwood, he gave a key to Quentin to watch the property."

Ariel put down her spoon and shook her head. "Two murders in the same year. It's surreal."

"It's still not as bad as Vancouver. And at least it's not a local person this time. It just happens to be local. I could've walked."

He saw the flashing lights of Ray's cruiser and gave Ariel a quick kiss. "See you later, Babe," and ran out the door.

"What a drag," she said to the cats. "I wanted us to go for a long walk today … maybe to the estuary or fish hatchery." She poured a second cup of coffee. *I'll call Lana. See if she wants to go to the Farmer's Market.* She noticed the time and wondered if it was too early to call. Then she thought her gal pal might be otherwise engaged. Not for the first time she was thinking what a monkey wrench Stefano Moretti had thrown into their friendship. She rarely saw Lana anymore. Annika and Sara then came to mind. She knew it wouldn't be too early for them as Maisie needed her morning walk. She picked up the phone. Annika was delighted with the idea.

Ariel had already decided not to say a word to them about the murder and hoped the radio station hadn't gotten wind of it. Her friend would find out soon enough and she didn't want to spoil the day, which was turning out to be crisp and sunny.

Quentin Pickell stood with the driver as they waited for the arrival of the authorities. "By the way. If you don't want to be pilloried by the police, you'd better keep your cellphone turned off and in your pocket."

"But I have to notify the company! We're supposed to start filming at eight o'clock."

"Young man, I've had enough experience with the Chief of Police to know that if you let the cat out of the bag, you'll be in deep doo-doo. This has to be kept quiet until they give you the say-so."

"Oh, crap. They're probably thinking we've been in an accident, or something."

"Better that than murder. So, let's just wait for everyone to arrive, shall we?" He steered him farther along the sidewalk.

The driver felt his phone vibrating for the dozenth time. Although he was itching to tell *someone* what had happened, he took the undertaker's advice. It wasn't long before a black and white pulled up and an imposing man in full uniform stepped out. The undertaker excused himself, engaged in a brief conversation with the man, who then walked over to the driver.

"I'm Chief of Police Wyatt. I understand you work for *Paradise Pines*?"

"Y-yes." His mouth felt like it was filled with cotton batting.

"I need you to get in touch with whoever's in charge. He needs to be informed.

"Uh, right. Okay." As he reached into his jacket pocket for his mobile, Wyatt stopped him.

"This is what you say. There's been an accident. Mr. Nygaard is dead and we're investigating the cause. That's all. Understood?"

"Understood, sir."

Wyatt nodded and returned to his vehicle. The driver pulled out his cellphone, glanced at the long list of messages then called Peggy Brotman, the Assistant to the Producer. As he relayed the scant information and listened to her shocked response, he watched officers and paramedics pouring from their vehicles, donning personal protective equipment and entering the house. Pulling up in a van, two plain-clothesmen got out.

He heard Peggy nattering in his ear. "Peggy. I can't tell you any more than that. Just call everybody. Okay? I have to go now." He hit the end icon and turned when he heard a deep rumbling sound. It was a Mobile Crime Vehicle. He had seen them on TV shows and was impressed that a small town would have such a rig.

A short officer in uniform swiftly placed yellow tape around the area and orange cones on the street. He stopped what he was doing as a bright red SUV pulled up. A woman alighted, went to the back of her vehicle, extracted a large package and began putting on her PPE. Once done, she picked up her medical bag and headed for the house. The driver thought she could have been plucked from central casting so perfect was she for the role of a modern-day coroner–a beautiful female of colour. He watched the police chief intercept her, say a few words, then stand staring at her as she entered the house.

Soon, neighbours were out gawking at the goings on, but were kept at bay by another uniformed officer as large as a linebacker. Standing next to the little cop, he created a scene so comedic that the driver momentarily forgot that an actual murder had taken place. Reality soon smacked him in the face when another officer approached him.

"I understand you were first on the scene," she said, flipping open a small notebook.

He gaped at her. *Wow! Another beauty.* Was she an Indian, or as they were told to call them, First Nations? He had never met one before. "Yes … yes, I was," he stammered.

"Could I have your name, please?"

He told her.

"Could you spell that, please?"

When he did, she didn't bat an eye. "Why were you here so early?"

He explained his job and early morning order.

"You were filming today?"

"Yes, at a house near the beach."

"Have you informed someone of the death of Nygaard?"

Upon hearing the words, his legs became wobbly. "Is he really dead?"

"You saw him, didn't you?" Her tone implied that he was some kind of jerk.

"Yes. That was a stupid thing to ask. Obviously he was dead. But I've never seen a dead person before. Only on screen. And then of course, they aren't really dead, are they?" He was becoming a blithering idiot.

She ignored him. "So, did you notify them, or not?"

Ooh. Think I've just been bitch slapped. "Yes, the police chief told me to call the Assistant to the Producer … well he didn't know who I was supposed to call, but that's who it was. She has the contact list for everyone. So she was to tell them not to leave town because Mr. Nygaard had died under suspicious circumstances."

She lasered him a look. "Are you sure that's what he said?"

"Well, uh, not exactly. He said there was an accident and Mr. Nygaard was dead and they were investigating."

She nodded. "That sounds more like it. Now, would you please give me a timeline of the events from when you first arrived."

He gave her what he could remember.

"Thank you. And I need your contact number in case we need additional information." After he repeated it, she told him to wait for a few minutes as another officer would be talking to him.

Damn! This would make a great police drama! he thought as she walked off. And she'd be the hard-assed bad cop.

While the forensic team got on with their work, Wyatt spoke to Jimmy. "I've got to alert Robyn. People from the neighborhood may be calling the station already. And I need to get Marina Davidova up to speed. Everyone in that television company will be posting the news on their social media sites and calling TV stations. With a story like this, it won't take long before we're deluged with inquiries." He slid into the car and picked up the phone.

Jimmy walked over to listen in on his partner's q and a with the undertaker.

Ray once again thought how much Pickell resembled his initials–Q.P.–a kewpie doll with a round head, big eyes and a tuft of hair atop a bald head. "So, Kewpie, I understand that you were second on the scene."

Quentin Pickell sighed and glowered at Ray. The undertaker didn't know which he hated worse–being called "Kewpie" or pickle, rather than Pickell. "Yes, that's correct. I heard someone banging on Nygaard's door and yelling. It was early."

"What time would you say?"

"Two minutes after seven." Ray almost smiled at the man's preciseness.

"And it continued?"

"Yes. So I got the key that Gordon Greenwood left me. He asked me to keep watch over the house when it was empty, but he didn't retrieve it after Nygaard moved in. And I got a flashlight because it was still pretty dark out. I went over to see what all the kerfuffle was about." He then related his movements inside the house.

"Anything else to add to that?"

"Only that with the breaker being off it was cold in the house. So no doubt that's going to affect rigor. But at least you have the approximate time of death."

"That's very fortunate for us, Mr. Pickell," Jimmy said.

The man turned to him with a smile. "How nice of you to pronounce my name correctly. I appreciate it."

The dig to Ray bounced off his back. "Anything else you can tell us?"

"Yes. I believe it began last night, actually."

"Really? What makes you think that?" Ray asked.

"I was watching TV when I heard three sharp noises. They were loud and very fast ... sort of like firecrackers attached together. You know the kind I mean."

"What time was that?"

"At approximately nine forty-five. I wondered if it was fireworks at the beach or some kids close by setting off fire crackers. I looked outside. Didn't see anyone. But I noticed that all the lights were out at Nygaard's, so I thought he was in bed. I finished watching the film and retired. From what I now know, I think they were the gunshots that killed Mr. Nygaard."

"Any other surprises up your sleeve, Quentin?" Ray asked with a smile.

Pickell remained stony faced. "No. I believe you have everything. I imagine I can go now. "

"Yes. With the usual caveats," Jimmy said.

"I understand." Pickell nodded and left.

Ray smirked. "He's one for the books. Almost precious."

"Now Ray," Jimmy chided.

Foxcroft came up to them, the driver in her wake. "This is the crew member who was first on the scene. I've got notes." She handed them to Ray who handed them to Jimmy.

"Thanks, Tamsyn."

"So ... what do you want me to do now?"

"What would you like to do?"

"Go home and have a big breakfast."

"Okay. Knock yourself out," Ray said.

"Really?"

"Sure. We've got it covered."

She saluted him, although what she did wasn't regulation. Ray and Jimmy cracked up.

Ray turned to the driver. "What's your name?"

"Angel Arellano." He said, and then spelled it out. Ray snatched the notes from Jimmy. "This says 'Angel'. Is that how you pronounce angel? *Anhel?*"

The driver laughed. "That's right. Anyone who doesn't live in Southern California probably wouldn't know that."

"The double el I get." Then he repeated the name. "Has a nice ring to it. Okay. So let's get down to business, Angel. First of all, why did Nygaard set up such a phantasmagoric display here?"

Jimmy broke out into a laugh.

"What's so funny, Tan?"

"I don't think I need to explain that," Jimmy replied. "I'm going inside now."

At this point, the driver was thinking sitcom.

Ray turned back to him, waiting for an answer.

"Umm. Well, I think he wanted something that the locals would like because we had some bad press. He was hoping it would change people's opinions 'cuz we're gonna be here for a while."

"You are? Won't this shut it down?" Ray asked.

"Are you kidding? With the amount of money sunk into it already? No way. As soon as they hear that Nygaard is dead, they'll be scrambling to find someone to fill his spot."

"What's your job?"

"I'm a gopher."

"Gopher?"

"Go for this. Go for that. You know. Do things that nobody else has time for … or wants to do."

"Doesn't sound very glamorous," Ray said.

Arellano snorted. "To tell you the truth, there isn't much glamour working in TV."

"Any ideas who might have murdered him?"

"Murdered. Jeez. No. Nobody here. At least I can't think of anyone."

"Nobody *here* as opposed to somewhere else?" Ray asked.

Arellano held up both hands. "No. No. That's not what I meant."

"Any friction on the set?"

"A bit. Always is during a shoot. But it's usually a professional spat of some kind. Nothing serious enough for murder."

"You never know," Ray said. "We'll be interviewing everyone."

"Oh boy. That will really screw up the shooting schedule."

"Uh huh. I imagine a little old thing like a murder isn't *nearly* as important as a shooting schedule," Ray said caustically.

"I'm sorry. I didn't mean that."

"Welcome to the real world, Angel."

"Should I tell the production team I saw the body? I know they're going to ask me that."

"Just say you saw it lying on the floor. But you were hustled away by the neighbour. That's all true, isn't it?"

'Yes."

"Well, that's all you tell them. No details. No doubt you could sell your story to some tabloid, but that has to wait until we find the perpetrator."

It hadn't occurred to Arellano to sell his story. But maybe when he got back to Hollywood …

Ray saw the excitement flare in his eyes. "By the way, you'll have to come in to the police station for a formal interview." That oughta take some of wind out of his sails, Ray thought. He allowed the driver to leave and joined the team.

Fourteen

H ave you noticed that the three murders we've had have all been on weekends?" Tim Novak, Corporal and Scene of Crime Officer, said to no one in particular.

"Yeah. You would think the killer would be more considerate," Ray said, while crouching beside the Medical Examiner and the decaying corpse. "So, what've we got here, Dr. D.?"

"Three shots from a medium caliber pistol. Probably nine millimeter," she replied. She hadn't minded that he hadn't called her by either of her names. Several years back it had been decided by Chief Wyatt that Dayani Nayagam was too difficult for him to get his mouth around, thus giving her the nickname. It stuck, and almost the entire criminal community had adopted it.

"Pickell said he thought they were loud firecrackers in quick succession. That would fit with a fully automatic handgun."

"Those are illegal here," Dhillon said.

"Uh huh. Everything's illegal here," Ray said.

"But they can be converted," SOCO Josh Atkins said, while erecting the equipment to determine the trajectory of the bullets and blood spatter pattern.

Novak and Dhillon had set up a grid searching for shell casings and come up empty, adding a touch of mystery to the murder.

She carefully cut open Nygaard's shirt and pants and examined the puncture holes, noting the "tattooing" of the burned gunpowder as it made contact with his skin.

Ray observed the entry holes–round and almost aligned. There was a reddish-brown abrasion on the inverted edges of the wound. "Looks like the perp and vic weren't that far apart."

"There's a void in the BSP where the perp was standing," Atkins said.

"It appears that the bullets may have penetrated the body," Dr. D. agreed.

Atkins pointed to the hallway wall. "They're here. Or what's left of them."

Novak took a spiral saw from his kit and began cutting through the plaster to retrieve the lodged bullets. When he was done, he placed the chunk in a plastic bag and tagged it. "Well, at least we have the bullets even though there are no casings," he said.

After Dr. D. collected the necessary samples, she turned to McDaniel. "Have you got all the photos we need of this side?"

"Yes." He put aside his camera and helped her carefully turn over Nygaard's body.

"Oh, this is interesting," she said in a voice that had everyone's attention. She spoke into her recorder. "Victim has fashioned a bandage on the back of his head." She removed a couple of adhesive bandages holding a piece of gauze in place. "Victim has a laceration on the back of his head." She positioned her cellphone by the wound. "It measures five centimeters by seven centimeters. That's only a close approximation. I'll get a better reading at the morgue after I've cleaned it up."

"So, he fell, or was pushed?" Ray asked, rhetorically.

"But there aren't any sharp edges around here," Jimmy said, looking around the entrance to the hall.

McDaniel scrolled through his log of photographs and found the picture they needed. "Here. On the side of the coffee table." They inspected the spot where Nygaard's head had made contact. Dr. D. collected samples of the hair and blood.

"Well, this gives us something else to think about," Ray said.

She continued with her examination, detailing the exit wounds. Close to finishing, she spied a thin black thread on the left side of Nygaard's neck. She pointed it out to Ray. "I'm going to have the lab analyze this."

"Okay."

Dropping it into an evidence bag, she then had Dhillon draw a chalk outline around the body, which the paramedics wrapped, loaded onto a gurney and wheeled out. "Okay, boys, I think I have everything I need here."

Wyatt was waiting to escort her out.

"Somehow, I don't think that's what she meant," Novak said under his breath. The men smiled.

Jimmy had left to walk around the house doing a cursory search. The room which interested him most was filled with desks and chairs, a storyboard tacked onto a cork board leaning on a giant easel, and a variety of digital equipment, computers, and four monitors. Four memory sticks, a larger mobile storage device and a cellphone were on a desk along with a piece of partially eaten pizza on a paper plate. Beside it was a half-empty bottle of water. *Was Nygaard working on the computer when the killer arrived?*

In the bedroom, he opened drawers, rifled through linen, checked under the bed, inspected closet shelves and turned out jacket and pants pockets. A khaki vest had been hung on the back of a chair. In one of the several pockets he found a folded piece of paper. He opened it up. What he saw puzzled him: the names of crew members and their job titles. The worn creases indicated that it had been unfolded and refolded many times. *Was Nygaard having trouble remembering their names?*

In the bathroom, among the medications for muscle pain and headaches, he found two drugs for sleep deprivation: over-the-counter Melatonin and a prescription bottle of Ativan. He bagged and tagged them and included the mouth wash, in case it was "dope water," then hit the kitchen.

Except for a half-dozen boxes of pizza and vacuum-wrapped beef patties in the freezer, the refrigerator was empty of food; only condiments for hot dogs and hamburgers, a box of milk and bottles of water and cans of soda, cases of which were stacked against a kitchen wall. In a tall pantry-style cupboard, Jimmy found bags of coffee beans, cans of chili con carne, and big bags of sugar, buns, and popped and flavoured popcorn. One cupboard beside the stove contained butter, salt and pepper, a sugar bowl and a few other condiments. It was the other one that caught Jimmy's attention. Here were bottles of various vitamins and other supplements, among them gingko biloba and turmeric. To him, they seemed out of place among the fast foods. He would pass them along to the lab for analysis.

A coffee bean grinder and French press sat on the counter. *So he eats junk but drinks a well-made cup of coffee and takes vitamins. Strange.* The sink was empty but the dishwasher was nearly full. On the table sat three-quarters of the pizza and a clean paper plate. *Was Nygaard expecting someone?"*

Returning to the living room, he spoke to Novak. "Did you find any pizza crumbs in this room?"

"Nope."

"Pack up the computers, mobile storage units and cellphone. Here's a piece of paper I found in a vest pocket that looks interesting. It'll need to be analyzed for prints. Gene can do that. I've bagged and tagged the medications and liquids in the bathroom. They're on the counter."

"Okay. I'll get Heppner to help. He's just sitting on his ass in the MCV," Novak snickered.

Jimmy nodded toward the back of the house. "It looks like people gathered in the room where all the electronics are. This house has been visited several times. I don't think taking prints will be a good use of your time." He smiled at the signs of relief on the faces of Novak and Dhillon. "But we'll take them at the station." He turned to Ray. "I'm ready for breakfast."

"You mean lunch."

As they walked down the steps, they saw a car from the local radio station. Then a reporter from *The Bayside Bugle* rushed up to them. "Hi, officers. Can I–"

"Can't give you anything, Nate. You'll have to talk to Chief Wyatt," Ray said, not breaking his stride.

"Isn't this where Berens Nygaard is staying?"

Ray wanted to say "was," but bit his tongue. "Call the station." They got into the van and drove away, dodging a few rubberneckers too close to the driveway.

Fifteen

Wyatt was correct. By the time he arrived at the station, Robyn Lewitski, the weekend dispatcher/receptionist, had already been fielding calls, giving out the standard spiel.

In the incident room, McDaniel was in the process of taping photographs on the white board. The smell of coffee and food floated in from the kitchen. Squad members settled in to hear Chief Wyatt's synopsis of the murder so far.

"Okay. This is what we've got. First of all, no shell casings were found, which leads us to believe the perpetrator knew what he was doing. Now, before anyone jumps on me for saying 'he,' I'm just going to say that it makes things easier than always saying 'he or she.' The gun was most probably a nine millimetre. Second, according to Kewpie, the breaker switch had been turned off. So the perp either knew where to find it or took the time to find it, which means that he was one cool customer."

A few of them broke into smiles. The Chief was famous for his use of cop clichés from old movies.

"I'm of the opinion that he knew where it was. So it's most probably someone from the production company who'd been in the house before. No reason for a local person to kill Nygaard. He was a stranger here. Hadn't had enough time to make enemies yet."

"Except for Delilah Moore and Vivian Hoffmeyer," Novak said, eliciting guffaws from a few.

Wyatt continued. "The only wrinkle so far is that Dr. D. found a large welt on the back of his head. As you can see from these photos, the side of the coffee table has blood on it. Obviously it had to have occurred before he was shot. His body was found several feet away. He looked around for comments. Being none, he carried on.

"So, did he fall or did someone push him? If so, why didn't that person shoot him then and there? And how long had the perp been inside the house? It was Hallowe'en, and kids would've been coming until, say, six o'clock or so. By then they're usually on their way to the Community Centre. So was the shooter there while Nygaard was handing out the candies? That would imply that Nygaard didn't suspect him ... or her. Or did the perp arrive afterwards? Are we looking at two separate people?"

"Kewpie said he heard the shots around nine forty-five and assumed they were fireworks. He saw lights out at Nygaard's and thought he was in bed," Ray said.

"Can we assume it was the perp at this point?" McDaniel asked.

"Makes sense," Wyatt replied.

"But can we also assume it was someone from the production company who killed him?" Novak asked.

"No," Jimmy was quick to say. "There are always variables, unknowns. And the fact that he arrived here with some nasty baggage adds to that. After we interview everyone from the company, we may have a better idea who it might be."

Wyatt looked at his watch. "On that note, we have everyone coming in shortly. I can't believe how many people are involved in making a TV show. Jimmy and Ray will do the interviews using both rooms. That way we can get through them faster. If we don't have time for all of them today, we'll have to continue tomorrow. McDaniel will get their prints. So let's see what we've got at the end of the day. In the meantime, I'm going to get on to the radio station and put out a PSA."

He got himself a cup of coffee and wrote down what he was going to say, then he figured Marina would be the perfect person to do that. She was as terse as he was, but used politer terms. He went to find her.

Goodbody was still in his pajamas and robe, sitting at the kitchen table, a cup of coffee going cold. He had put on the radio listening for news, wondering if the death of Nygaard would be announced. It was not.

Then the station interrupted its regular program. "We have a Public Service Announcement from the Britannia Bay Police Department. They are asking for the public's help in the suspicious death that took place last evening on Hyacinth Road. We would like anyone who saw or heard anything unusual between the hours of six and ten o'clock to contact the police." He then gave the number.

There it was. Filled with foreboding and regret, Goodbody replayed the scene, something he had been doing throughout the night. It was an accident, but the man was dead. He had to go to the police and confess. If he did that, he would be saving them a lot of work. And the television company could get on with the business of filming again. Or would they leave? The town and local businesses would lose a lot of money. People would be put out of work. Oh, my Lord. What have I done? But at least that bastard is dead!

Keith Kittridge's fork froze between the plate and his mouth as he listened to the PSA. *Suspicious death my ass. Murder is more like it!* "Crikey! Edith!" he shouted as he jumped up from the table and hurried into the bedroom, where his wife was changing to go out.

"What's the matter? Are you all right?"

He waved his hands in front of him. "No. No. It's not me. I'm fine. Edith, there's been another murder!"

"Oh, no! Not another one? Who is it?"

"I think it's that director from *Paradise Pines*. Nygram."

"Nygaard," she corrected him. Berens Nygaard."

"Whatever. That foreigner. They're already asking for the public's help."

"Did they give his name? They don't usually."

"No. But they said Hyacinth Road and I happen to know that that's where he is living. Or was. Nate tracked him down when he arrived in town." He turned as though to leave then turned back. "I've gotta call Wyatt. This is going to be a media circus, Edith. You think Berdahl's murder brought in the press? Well, wait until the Americans hear about this. We'll have CNN and FOX and ABC and all the other acronyms on the planet sending stringers here. Not to mention all the other pseudo news sites on the Internet. Holy kadodie. It's going to be a real show. Marina Davidova will be a star!"

"Listen to yourself, Keith. You sound like it's a good thing."

"Well, it isn't a bad thing, Edith. What's the loss of one has-been director who was a druggie and a womanizer?"

"It could shut down the production and Britannia Bay would lose that money."

"They won't shut it down, Edith. It'll get ratings like you won't believe. There's nothing like a scandal to titillate an audience. Now, I've gotta get a move on," and he rushed out as fast as he had rushed in.

Edith shook her head. For her husband, it was another good "bad news" day. But for her, it was the words of John Donne: *Any man's death diminishes me.*

Marina Davidova sat with Wyatt discussing the upcoming press conference. "It's going to be a shit storm. I hope we have something before Tuesday," he said. "Maybe this PSA will elicit some responses. I imagine we'll have all the national news stations descending on us."

"Including the French one. Don't forget about them."

Wyatt raised his eyes heavenward. "How could I ever forget Mademoiselle Marie Dee-ann Goudron. She was one piece of work."

"I heard she was fired right after she filed that report … even though it was true."

"Well, good."

"Now you'll have to get prepared for some Americans, too."

"If they can find us," he laughed.

The intercom buzzed. "Keith Kittridge is here to see you, Chief."

Wyatt smiled. "Speaking of the press," he whispered to Marina. "Okay. Tell him to come on back."

"You're going to talk to him?" Marina's surprise filled her face.

"I'm going to give *him* the scoop. And the local radio station. Why should the big guys get all the goodies?"

Keith bustled into Wyatt's office, all fired up. "Good of you to see me, Bill. Hi there, Marina. How're you doing?"

"Holding up," she smiled.

Keith appraised the beautiful Russian. "Yes, I can see that," he said, wryly.

"Now, Keith ..." she mocked him.

"Right. So, what've you got for me?"

"Not much ... but you're getting it first," Wyatt said.

"I could've sworn that was a threat," he chuckled.

Sixteen

Sunday, November 2nd

By the time they were called in for interviews, everyone from *Paradise Pines* had been informed that Berens Nygaard's death was not an accident, but murder. Peggy Brotman was first up, and Robyn wasn't sure she was who she said she was being young and very tiny.

"You're Peggy Brotman?" she asked.

Brotman laughed. "Yeah, I get that all the time."

"I'll buzz you in. You'll be fingerprinted first then interviewed by Detective Sergeant Jimmy Tan, who will be taking your statement."

"Oh. Fingerprinted? Hmm. I guess I should have expected that." She shrugged. "Okay."

As she trailed behind Robyn, all eyes were on the diminutive woman with a light brown Afro. Under a short black leather jacket, her tight jeans revealed a completely flat rear end. Spying a room filled with men, she broke into a broad smile, displaying a mouth full of bright, tiny teeth.

"Well, if she's the perp, then she's Wyatt's really cool customer," Novak said.

Robyn introduced Brotman to Gene McDaniel. He looked down at her. She looked way up at him. They shared a smile as though sharing similar thoughts. Other than the dissimilarity in their heights, hers might have been his colour; his, her Afro. After he took her prints, he led the way to an interview room where he introduced her to Jimmy.

"Oh, hello," she greeted him warmly. "You're the one who called me."

"That's right."

"Nice to meet you." She took in the room. "This isn't as sterile as I thought it would be."

"This is what we call a soft interview room. It's for people who aren't under arrest." Gesturing to a chair, he politely told her to take a seat. When she removed her jacket, Jimmy found it difficult not to do a double take. He swiftly focused his attention on his notes.

In the observation room, Novak, who was recording the interview, had to figuratively pick up his jaw from the floor.

"This is such a pretty little town. I'll bet you don't get many murders here," she said, making herself comfortable.

Jimmy sensed that she liked to chatter, so he cut short any further attempts at social conversation. "Thankfully, no. Now, let's begin." He asked the usual introductory questions. The only answer that surprised him was her age—thirty. Was her youthfulness down to a face bereft of makeup? "How long have you worked on this production?"

"Right from the beginning. We did a pilot about two years ago, and it generated a lot of interest. Much more than we expected, as a matter of fact. So we jumped right into the series production. This is the second season and the first one on location."

"How did you get hired?"

"Strictly being in the right place at the right time." Then she smiled. "And, of course, knowing the right people. That's key in this industry."

"Who hired you?"

"The Producer."

"Would that be Allen Benson?"

"No. Allen's the Line Producer." She gave the name of the Producer. Jimmy ran down the list. "His name is not here."

"No. He's back in Hollywood. Producers don't usually hang around a set."

"Oh, I see. So Mr. Benson oversees the details during the shoot."

"That's right."

"Have you worked with him before?"

"Yes. We did a Movie of the Week just before the pilot."

"Is he easy to work with?"

"Umm, he can be a bit intense because his responsibilities are huge. So I've learned how to be around him ... you know, when to back off. But I have to make him aware of certain problems that I know are going to piss ... I mean, upset him. But he has to know. You know?"

Jimmy nodded. "Now, I want to ask you some questions about Berens Nygaard. I know it's early in the investigation, but have you given any thought to who might be responsible for his death?"

"Well, a lot of women back in Hollywood would've gladly killed him," she tittered.

"That's not what I meant," Jimmy mildly admonished her.

She flushed. "I know. I'm sorry."

"But no one here. No one in the crew that you can think of?"

"In the crew?" She gave a nervous laugh trying to cover her shock. "No. Except for the head positions, most of them are from Vancouver. He might've known some of them from before, though, because he shot a movie there once."

"Did you stop in Vancouver on your way here?"

"Yes. I stayed for a couple of days. It's a gorgeous city. And so clean."

"It's the rain," he said, dryly.

"We could use some of it in L.A."

"How was his interaction with the cast and crew in general?"

"In many cases, he wasn't on a first-name basis with them. And it could be annoying when he pointed to someone and said something like 'you there' when he wanted their attention."

"Did he ever address you that way?"

She laughed. "No. He knows my name. There's only a few women, and we're all different. So I guess that makes it easy. Most of the guys look a lot alike and they dress alike, too, which doesn't help."

Jimmy made a mental note to check the list he had found in Nygaard's vest, then moved on.

"What about any tension between him and a particular cast or crew member?"

"The only person who seemed to get under his skin was Tiffany Blair, the lead."

"Do you happen to know why?"

"Yes, I do. She was always wanting to make changes in the script while we were shooting a scene. That caused delays, because they would get into arguments about it."

"Arguments? Not discussions?"

"No. Out-and-out shouting matches."

"That must have been uncomfortable for everyone."

"That's putting it mildly."

"Did Nygaard ever agree with her suggestions?"

"Sometimes. Sometimes she was right. The writing could be trite and old fashioned and not something her character would say."

"Okay. Now, when we searched the house, we found several flash drives."

"I'm guessing that those would be the rushes."

"Rushes?"

"The dailies. The unedited footage from the day's shooting. Nygaard and Nina Ortiz–she's the script supervisor–and maybe a couple of other relevant people would determine if any scenes needed reshooting. After they had been edited, Nygaard would send them electronically to Hollywood for post production."

"Can you give me a list of people who might be included?"

"Okay. Do you want that now?"

"You can email it to me later today. By any chance would you know the password to his computers?"

"I don't, but Allen might."

Jimmy jotted a note then continued. "Were you at Nygaard's on Hallowe'en evening?"

"No. I was at the beach."

"The whole evening?"

"Yes. I got there at around six thirty. A bunch of people had arrived already and they saved some places for everybody else."

"What time did you leave?"

"I'm guessing around ten thirty. I think most everyone had cleared out by then."

"You think?"

"Well I couldn't tell. It was pretty dark by then, even though the bonfire lit everything up. But we were spread out, too. We had originally been in a group, but by that time, we had sort of paired up with people we preferred, if you know what I mean."

He nodded his understanding. With all the details covered, Jimmy gave the time, ended the interview and thanked her.

When they walked back through the squad room, eyes nearly fell out of heads. Brotman had not yet put on her jacket.

Checking that neither Foxcroft nor Dussault were present, Carpenter said, "Well, that explains where her ass went."

"Lucky Novak. He got a full frontal for forty-five minutes," Drew Hastings said.

Ray hadn't seen this display, being busy interviewing Tiffany Blair. Her arrival had garnered a comment about Ray getting the breaks as she was exceptionally beautiful. But after she didn't even acknowledge them, they decided that Blair's svelte body and blonde good looks combined with Brotman's boobs and personality made up the perfect package.

Blair divulged a certain tension between Nygaard and Benson. Nygaard had once had a reputation for causing problems during a shoot, so she thought Benson was keeping him on a short leash. But questioned further, she said she was just thinking that that's what she'd do if she were Benson. Her mother was staying with her, and on Hallowe'en night they had dinner at their rental home and didn't go to the beach. She uttered not a word of her run-ins with the director.

After she left, Steve Brookside, the male star, was ushered in. He reminded Ray of a younger James Brolin and would be spinning heads if he ventured out onto the streets of town. After asking the usual questions, Ray realized that Brookside was not a player, did not like parties, and, when he wasn't on the set, spent his time with his first and only wife, who was pregnant. He had nothing to add to the mix.

Nina Ortiz, the Script Supervisor, was next. She told Ray she had been to Nygaard's house on Hallowe'en along with the Weapons Master, Cal Jackson.

"What time did you get there?"

"It was early. About 4:00."

"The filming had stopped by then?"

"Yes. We had a problem with the weapons not firing, so we couldn't continue the shoot. Berens wanted to review the footage to see if we could salvage the scene."

"The weapons misfired?"

"Yes."

Ray didn't pursue this with her. He would give this fact to Jimmy who could cover it with the Weapons Master.

"What did you do at Nygaard's house?"

"We watched the scene, decided it had to be reshot, and left. Oh, and we passed out some of the Hallowe'en candy to the kids. They were already arriving by the time we left."

"What time was that?"

"About five-thirty."

"Did Nygaard have a bandage on the back of his head?"

She looked puzzled. "No."

"Do you have any idea as to why Mr. Nygaard was killed?"

She moved her head back and forth in bewilderment. "It hasn't really sunk in yet. I'm concerned about the continuation of the series. It's sad, though, because he was doing such a great job. We got along well. I'll miss him."

After she left, Ray found Jimmy. "Here's some information you need to have," and he told him about the misfiring weapons.

"Hmm. Might have some bearing on the case. Do you want to sit in on the interview?"

Ray checked his watch. "I have the big enchilada, Allen Benson, coming in in fifteen minutes. But I guess I can spare you my expertise until then."

"Okay, Mr. Big Shot. You lead off and I'll do damage control."

"Hah!"

Cal Jackson, the Weapons Master, strode in purposefully. Jimmy recognized a man with gravitas when he saw one. You didn't get to be in that position if you were a nervous Nellie. Tall, lean and ramrod straight, his faintly lined face and short brush cut showing grey among the brown put him a few years older than his fellow workers. He sat comfortably, clasping his hands in this lap, completely unfazed at being recorded.

"Mr. Jackson, could you tell us about the scenes in which the prop guns misfired?" Ray began.

"They are blank firing guns," he said laconically. "And what do you want to know?"

"Why they misfired," Ray answered as tersely.

"Dud ammunition in the first one. The second one jammed," he answered in a neutral tone.

"Who was firing them?"

"The actor portraying an intruder."

"Had he handled a gun before?"

"Probably not. He was Canadian."

Ray didn't miss the put down. "Did you coach him?"

"Yes. He was fine. It wasn't his fault."

"So the day's shoot was halted."

"That's right."

"How did that affect you?"

"I had to thoroughly clean the guns and replace the firing pin in the second one."

"What model would they be?"

"Glock 19 Gen 4."

"Why would you be using a blank firing gun rather than a replica?"

"Because it's more realistic. The sound of the shots are similar to real ones. And there's a muzzle flash."

"But they have cartridges, right?"

"Right. It's a blank cartridge, not a bullet. You have the casing—or shell, if you prefer—gunpowder, then a primer at the bottom, and instead of a bullet, the tip is crimped—sealed—with either paper wadding or wax to hold in the gunpowder. So when you pull the trigger, you get the bang, muzzle flash, and an ejected shell, just like the real thing."

"Where are these guns stored?"

"In a safe in my room. And if you want to know, it's accessed with both a combination and a key. They never go near the set unless I'm carrying them."

"Did you take them to Nygaard's house that afternoon?"

"No. I didn't need to. Plus, I don't make a habit of travelling with them." While his voice remained flat, his mouth indicated the merest twitch of criticism.

Feeling bile rising, Ray took a beat to prevent himself from biting off his next comment. "But he would have wanted to know that they were in firing condition for tomorrow."

"Yes. I explained to him what I did, that I tested them and they were in good working order."

"And he was satisfied with that?"

"He was."

"Do you know if Mr. Nygaard had a gun?"

"He did."

If Ray and Jimmy were startled, they concealed it.

"Did you ever see it?"

"I not only saw it, I cleaned it."

This caused them further consternation.

"What model was it?"

Jackson assessed them. "It's a Glock 19, Gen 4. But if you're asking that question, I'm assuming you didn't find it."

"No. We haven't found it yet," Jimmy said, without blinking.

"But a search of the premises is still ongoing," Ray said, compounding the lie. "It seems odd that the guns used in the production and Mr. Nygaard's are the same. How did this come about, or do you know?"

"It was his decision. When he selected the gun for the shoot—no pun intended—I had no idea that he would be acquiring the same model for himself somewhere along the line."

"Do you have any idea where he got it?"

"No. I only know that he didn't have it when we left the U.S."

"Did you stop over in Vancouver?"

"No. I was only at the airport to change planes."

"Back to the evening of the murder. What time did you get to Nygaard's house?"

"At sixteen hundred hours."

They were taken aback by his use of the 24-hour clock.

"And you left when?"

"At seventeen-thirty hours.

"Did you see anyone around his house, or a car you recognized or anything suspicious?"

"No. But I wasn't looking for anything like that."

"What did you do after that?"

"I went to dinner with Nina Ortiz. Directly after that I returned to my room and racked out."

"Mr. Jackson, do you have any idea why Mr. Nygaard was killed?"

For the first time, he hesitated before answering. "I've thought about that. I knew this production meant a lot to him. When it started up, he was relaxed. Happy, even. But as the shoot continued, he seemed to lose some of his faculties. Since arriving here, he's been tense, jumpy. Focusing on the team like a fox outside a henhouse. It bordered on the paranoid."

"Any conjecture as to why?"

"I have no idea."

"What was your experience with guns before joining the production?"

"I was a United States Marine."

Ray smothered a smile.

Jimmy wrapped up the interview.

As Jackson left, he gave a salute. Unlike Foxcroft's rude representation, his was the genuine article.

"A fucking Marine!" Ray laughed. "Well, our luck he didn't come to our rescue."

"He did give us a couple of things though–Nygaard's gun and his mood change."

"I'm betting Nygaard picked up the Glock in Vancouver. Easy enough to come by if you know the right people."

"It could be the gun that killed him."

"That would mean the perp knew he had a gun and knew where he kept it. Who would know that?"

"Well, it seems a lot of people were in and out of that house," Jimmy said. "Anyone could have taken an opportunity to do a bit of sniffing around when Nygaard was busy showing dailies to whomever."

Ray took a minute to check out the fair-skinned man with thinning hair and thickening girth seated in front of him. Wyatt had unwittingly dubbed him "the big enchilada" and it appeared to be an appropriate appellation. When he replied to questions, his speaking voice was soft and pleasant. His dark eyes, however, were sharp and penetrating. Overall, Allen Benson radiated a sense of restrained power.

Ray asked him about Nygaard's past. "We've been told that he was a bit of a philanderer."

Benson didn't smile, but it was there. "You're being kind."

Ray chuckled. "Can you give me some background?"

"He played around a lot and was known to take risks."

"How so?"

"He thought he was Mr. Teflon but he was finally caught with the wife of a powerful and dangerous man. And apparently he was in possession of drugs. Some favours were called in and Nygaard found himself out of work."

"Was he charged with possession?"

"Yes, but he said they were planted by some *associates* of the man."

Ray understood the emphasis Benson placed on the word. "What happened to the charges?"

"They were dropped."

"So what was the point of that?"

"No doubt to scare him."

"Why do you think he was hired for *Paradise Pines*?"

"The Executive Producer needed a name for the pilot. Nygaard still had name recognition. Good or bad." He lifted his hands. "And here we are."

"Did the fact that he had name recognition impress you?"

Again, that hint of humour behind his eyes. "I've worked with enough assholes not to get overwhelmed by their press. And he was no longer an important personality in Hollywood."

Ray launched right into the next question, "Do you happen to have the password to either of his computers?"

Benson didn't blink. "Yes. I have it for one but not the other." He gave the simple password without asking why it was needed.

Ray wrote it down. "What were you doing on Hallowe'en night?"

"Watching an old movie in my room."

"You didn't go to the beach?"

"I see enough of those people all day long. And that's not my idea of fun. I enjoy my own company."

"Was the movie on television?"

Benson smiled. "Now you're going to check to see if the film I was watching was being aired." It was a statement, not a question. "I'm sorry to disappoint you, but it's on one of the DVDs I carry around with me."

"What is it, if you don't mind me asking?"

"It's 'Young Frankenstein'."

Ray smiled. "My daughter is obsessed with that movie. Does impersonations from it, left, right and centre."

"It's a classic."

"Mr. Benson, do you own a gun?"

The abrupt question altered Benson's demeanour. "Yes, I do. But it's in my house in L.A."

"Do you mind telling me what kind it is?"

"It's a Ruger LCR .38 Special."

Ray nodded. "Those are good for home protection."

"That's why I got it."

"Do you know if Nygaard owns a gun?"

"Yes. More than one, so I understand."

"Do you know if he was in possession of a gun here?"

"Yes, I do know that. He made no secret about it."

That answered one of their questions. "Do you know where he got it?"

"No. But my guess is that he picked it up in Vancouver because he wouldn't have been able to get it past the border guards." This time he smiled, which altered his face, making him almost handsome. "Our Weapons Master said they opened the crate carrying the two prop weapons and almost confiscated them."

Ray chuckled. "That good are they?"

"Yes. We try to be as accurate as possible."

Ray glanced down at his notes. "Did you notice any personality change in Nygaard since arriving here?"

"Like what?"

"His moods or a change in his relationship with the crew, for example."

"The only thing I noticed was that he seemed to be absent minded. No. Strike that. Losing his train of thought was more like it. And it made him angry. Sometimes it would put people on edge. Any little thing touched him off. But he was under a lot of pressure … some of it self-imposed."

"I don't imagine it's good for the production that he was killed."

"Well, there are two thoughts about that. On the one hand it could be bad because it'll delay the shoot and increase our costs. On the other, the publicity might generate a larger audience and ad revenues. So you never know how it's going to play out."

Ray nodded. "Any idea who will replace him?"

Benson shook his head. "Haven't a clue."

After he left, Wyatt and Jimmy asked what he got from him.

"Well, other than the password to one of the computers he was rather abstemious with his information."

Wyatt and Jimmy cracked up.

"Now who's the resident wordsmith?" Wyatt ribbed him.

"Yeah, well, Tan's not the only one with a copy of Funk and Wagnalls."

"It just doesn't suit you, Ray," Wyatt said, still smiling.

By late afternoon, everyone had been interviewed. Robyn had explained the routine to her replacement when her shift was over. Jacquie was sorry that she had missed the stars. She had heard that the male lead was some kind of gorgeous. "What was he like?" she asked Robyn.

"Bland," she answered flatly.

Seventeen

Delilah sat with two parishioners in the church basement having a cup of tea and a piece of carrot cake. "I can't imagine where it is," she said for the third time. "I'm sure I had it on when I was passing around the candy on Hallowe'en. But I just can't remember when I last saw it."

"At our age, our fingers get bony, Delilah. And rings get to be too big. It may have slipped off when you were doing the dishes in soapy water."

"I have a thingy in the drain so it wouldn't have gone down there." She took another bite of the cake. "It's not in any of the places where you would expect it to be–not in the garbage or any of the wastebins. I even looked in Tabitha's bag of food and in her bed."

"Well, the best thing to do is to pray," suggested one.

"In my experience, taking a nap can help," advised the other. "Things come to us in our sleep and we wake up with the solution. So try taking a nap."

Delilah thought they were both good ideas, so later on that day, she combined the two. She laid back on her pink recliner, covered herself with her pink crocheted throw, and closed her eyes. "Dear Lord Jesus, I know you are awfully busy, as usual, but I need your help. I have lost my wedding ring. It's so precious to me. Melvin bought it on a layaway when he was young and poor. He got it in time for the wedding, though. It's gold with a small diamond in the centre and a teeny diamond on each side. It would break my heart to lose it. So I'm asking for your help. I'm also going to ask Melvin. He sometimes watches over me and maybe he saw what happened to it. So I'm going to go to sleep now, and hope the answer will be waiting for me when I wake up. But, Lord, I won't be troubled if it isn't. Something will happen. I love you, Jesus." And she closed her eyes, feeling better already.

Ariel's plan not to mention the murder to Annika had quickly backfired. It had taken less than a half hour at the Farmer's Market before bits of chatter floated around them as they strolled from kiosk to kiosk taking in the fresh produce and hand-made crafts. Annika had pulled Ariel away from Sara, who was examining a display of miniature animals made of papier maché, and questioned her. Ariel admitted that a murder had happened the previous night and told her who it was. Annika was so visibly shaken that Ariel accompanied her to some chairs. Sara had come over when she saw her mother sitting down and asked if she was okay. Annika said she was all right, that she just needed something to drink. Sara brought her a glass of water, which made Annika want to cry.

Now she was on the phone to her husband. "Sara is absolutely traumatized. She wasn't fooled that I was all right. So when we got home I told her about the man being dead. Zack, we could have been among the last people to see him alive. There was a witch behind Sara and two boys coming up the street toward the house. I think we should tell the police what we saw."

"Why don't you wait until the police ask for the public's help? For all you know, they may already have a suspect in custody."

She understood his reasoning, but thought he was being too … what? NIMBYish? When she hung up, Sara sidled up to her. "Mommy?"

Annika put an arm around her and pulled her close. "What is it, darling?"

Sara's voice was small and fearful when she answered. "When I was getting my treats at that house, I smelled something. It was from behind me. From the witch."

"What did you smell, honey?"

"Mommy," She choked out and started to cry. "It was the patchouli. I think the witch was Jade."

In the incident room, Wyatt tossed around what they had learned, then waited for his crew's input.

"It's quite possible that Nygaard was shot with his own gun," Ray said.

"But how would the perp know where to find it?" McDaniel asked.

"Crew members had been at the house setting up the Hallowe'en display," Jimmy began. "They had to do that during daylight hours, so they must have had access to the house. Was Nygaard at home or on the set? If so, what about the security code? Did one of them have it, or did they wait for him to return home before they left? Maybe someone nosing around found it. He might not have been the perpetrator, but he could have mentioned it to someone."

"That kind of gossip is gold," McDaniel said.

"I'll reinterview one of the electricians and see if I can get more details."

"Maybe after Nygaard was hit on the head, he brought out the gun while he waited for whoever was coming to see him later on. You know, just as added protection," Novak said.

"Assuming that that's what he was doing," Ray said.

"I think Nygaard *was* waiting for someone. A pizza and a clean paper plate were on the kitchen table," Jimmy pointed out.

"Maybe during a struggle with Nygaard the killer grabbed the gun and shot him," Atkins said.

Individually, they imagined the scene. "Could have happened that way," Ray said. "There was burned gunpowder on his skin."

"In the meantime, everyone has an alibi," Wyatt said.

As daylight faded, they felt they were not much farther ahead. But they were certain about one thing: among all the interviews were not only omissions but outright lies. Until they had a bit more to go on, however, they didn't know where to start digging for them.

Eighteen

Monday, November 3rd

As soon as Annika heard the radio announcement for the public's help, she had called the station and set up an appointment for first thing Monday morning. Jimmy was waiting for her. "Thanks for coming in, Annika."

"You're welcome, Jimmy. I don't know how helpful my information may be."

"You never know. Anything that sheds the smallest light on a case is helpful." They had reached the door to the interview room. "We'll take your statement in here."

"Statement?" Her body tensed.

"Yes. It will be a formal interview, which means it will be recorded. And Chief Wyatt and my partner will be present as well."

"Oh. I thought we would just talk ... you know ... um ... just you and me, over coffee. My husband didn't even want me to come," she said.

"Why is that?"

"Because it involves Sara."

Jimmy sensed that she seemed to be getting cold feet and might bolt. "Don't worry. We won't need to talk to her."

"Oh, that's a relief. She's already distraught over what she thinks she knows."

Jimmy opened the door. Wyatt and Ray stood. "Mrs. Johansson, this is Chief Wyatt and my partner, D.S. Ray Rossini."

Ray smiled and offered his hand. "Good morning. Pleased to meet you."

Wyatt did the same, adding that they appreciated her coming forward. He pulled out the chair. "If you could just sit here."

Her eyes darted around the room.

"I'll start this interview with your name and address and the reason you are here."

After a few minutes, her interest overshadowed her apprehension. She took it all in knowing full well that Sara would want to know every detail.

"What prompted you to contact us, Mrs. Johansson?"

"It was something my daughter, Sara, said. First of all you need to know that she has a keen sense of smell. She was born with it. It's called hyperosmia. Fortunately, it's not an acute form of the condition, so she doesn't get migraines or suffer from depression. However, she does experience anxiety, and recognizes it in others. She's a sensitive child. Just recently we were visiting Jade Errington, and she had patchouli plants in her greenhouse. Sara didn't like the smell. When she was standing at Mr. Nygaard's door on Hallowe'en night, she smelled it. It was coming from a witch standing behind her."

"Were you standing with her?" Ray asked.

"No. I was at the end of the driveway."

"So you didn't smell it."

"No."

"Did you notice anything unusual about the witch?"

Annika thought for a moment. "I thought she was quite tall. So more like an adult than a child. Or a very tall teenager."

"You said 'she.' Did you think the witch was a female?" Wyatt asked.

"Well, they usually are," she said, grinning.

"You got me there," Wyatt chuckled. "Did you see the witch getting candy?"

"No. I was too focused on Sara. And I was concerned with the time. We had to get to the Community Centre for the costume competition. So I don't know what happened with the witch. But two boys were coming toward us, so they might have seen something."

"Two boys?"

"Their costumes were the kind boys wear, so I assumed they were boys."

"Did they have parents with them?"

"No. They were by themselves."

"So, teenagers, most likely. Do you remember their costumes?"

"One was dressed like a punk rocker with a blond wig and tiny guitar. And the other was some kind of character from *Star Wars*. He had one of those light sabers."

"How is Sara, Mrs. Johansson?" Jimmy asked.

"She's upset. She's afraid Jade is the witch and is in trouble. She likes her."

"A lot of people still wear patchouli. Tell her that."

"Thank you. I will."

"Thanks for coming in, Mrs. Johansson. You've been a big help."

Well, Zack, so much for your reticence, she thought.

After she left, Wyatt pointed to Jimmy. "Go talk to Jade. Don't frighten her. She's spooked enough by townsfolk. It may be nothing. I've got to get out another PSA right away on those two boys who may have witnessed something. If they don't come in right away, we'll put out a description of their costumes. That'll put a fire under their butts."

The sign said 'NO TRESPASSING!' and a high chain link gate on wheels covered the entrance to Jade Errington's property. Jimmy got out of the black and white and peered through the wire. How was he going to get inside to ask her some questions? Then he remembered that Ariel had her phone number. He pulled out his cellphone.

"Hi, honey," she answered. "What do you need?"

He laughed. "How well you know me. I need Jade Errington's phone number. I'm at her place and there's no way to get in."

"I'm not surprised. Just a sec." A minute later, she gave him the number. "What does your call display say?"

"J. Tan."

"Hmm. She may think it's me and answer. Good luck."

"Does she have a land line?"

"No. Just a cell."

"Okay. Thanks." He punched in the number and waited. When it went to message he said: "Miss Errington, It's Sergeant Tan and I'm at your gate. I need to speak with you about Hallowe'en night. Can you please open the gate?" No response. He checked his watch. Leaning against the car and putting his face up to the sun, he decided to enjoy the warmth of the day while he waited. He checked the time again. Five minutes had passed. He called again and repeated the message. No response. Perhaps she wasn't even home. Or, being a lovely day, she might be in the garden and didn't have her phone with her.

He jiggled the gate. The clanging racket might be enough to get her attention. He checked the lock. Check that. Locks. This was a woman who was not taking chances. *If I had my gun I could shoot all three of them open the way they do on cop shows.* He started to giggle.

"It might be funny to you, but it's upsetting my chickens." He looked up and saw Jade Errington standing with her hands on her hips.

'Oh, sorry, Miss Errington, but I was trying to make a noise to get your attention."

"Well, now that you've got it, what do you want? And who are you?"

"Sorry. I'm Detective Sergeant Jimmy Tan. I called your cellphone but you didn't answer."

"Are you Ariel's husband?"

"Yes."

Her rigid posture relaxed a bit. "What is it you want?"

"It's about a homicide that occurred on Hallowe'en night. I don't know if you've heard about it."

"I don't live in a cave, Officer Tan. I was at the Farmer's Market on Saturday morning and heard about a murder the night before. So why do you want to talk to me?"

"There may be a suspect, and a witness said he or she was wearing patchouli."

Jimmy could see her putting two and two together. But she bluffed. "What's that got to do with me?"

"We know you grow the plants and make patchouli oil. So we were wondering if you sold it to anyone."

"I do sell it, but I don't keep a list of the buyers. They pay cash. Who was the victim? Is it someone I know?"

"No. It's no one local."

"If it's no one local, then who cares?"

"It's still murder, Miss Errington. And we have to follow every lead we have, no matter how silly it seems."

"I suppose you do."

"Did you go out on Hallowe'en by any chance?"

"No. It's one night I make sure I'm home. Last year some yahoos smashed the one lock I had on my gate and began tipping over my hives until I caught them at it. I managed to save my bees. That's when I put three locks on the gate."

Jimmy thanked her and was glad he hadn't accused her of being the witch who broke into Nygaard's house and killed him.

The ringing of his phone jarred Percy out of his dark thoughts. It was Jade.

"Percy, the police have been here. We have to talk."

Nineteen

A re we all set for the press conference tomorrow?" Ray asked Wyatt. "With what little we've got, it's going to be a lot like the last one."

Wyatt laughed. "We pissed off a whole lot of people back then, didn't we? The only solid question we got was from that Francophone reporter. By the way, Marina tells me she was fired."

"Good. And so was the paramedic who tipped her off," Ray said.

"So I heard, and another French Canadian took his place."

"Yeah, but he's a straight shooter. Used to be Lana Westbrook's gardener."

"You don't say. So how did he come to be a paramedic?"

"He used to be one, back in Lac Megantic when that train rolled through town and exploded."

"Oh, shit."

"Yeah. Packed it in and came about as far from that place as you can get. Buried himself working with plants."

"Speaking of plants, at this point, the only things we've got are the little girl's smell of patchouli on the witch, and the two boys who were near the scene. We really lucked out there. Thank God people still listen to their radios around here." He noted the time. "If they're punctual, they should be here pretty soon."

They got up. "Jimmy's got an interview about now with a gaffer from the show," Ray began.

"What's a gaffer?"

"The head electrician, apparently."

"Gaffer. Gopher. For crying out loud. Why do they come up with these ridiculous names?"

"To speak in parables and separate themselves from the great unwashed."

Wyatt snorted, then asked why Jimmy was interviewing him.

"He was one of the guys putting up Hallowe'en decorations at Nygaard's house. Jimmy wants to know who all was involved."

"Okay. Keep me posted." He went over to Tamsyn. "Foxcroft, can you come with me to interview these boys? I want you to take notes. And it would help to have a woman present."

"Do you want me in on the questioning?"

"Only if you think I've overlooked something, but keep notes and if something strikes you, wait until we're nearly over, and ask it then."

"Okay. Thanks."

"I'm going to interview them in the Visitor's Room. It's more welcoming."

"Makes sense."

While waiting, Wyatt poured himself a cup of coffee and read the latest issue of *The Bayside Bugle*, rocking in his chair as he did so. He thought that Kittridge had done a good job—hadn't sensationalized the story but made it a bit titillating, mentioning Nygaard's sketchy past, intimating that there were a number of people who might want to see the end of him. *So, he had interviews of his own with the crew, eh? Good plan.* Wyatt learned nothing new from the article.

Mary Beth announced the boys' arrival. Wyatt made his way to the front, signaling for Foxcroft to join him. In the foyer, they saw two boys, big-eyed with curiosity. When they saw Foxcroft, they did a double take. Their parents were aware of the presence of a First Nations constable on the force and didn't give her more than a prudently veiled once-over.

After introductions were made, Wyatt said they would use the Visitor's Room. One boy asked, "Does it have a one-way mirror?"

Wyatt laughed. "I'm afraid not."

"Will we be videoed and recorded?" the other one asked.

One of the parents told the boys to behave.

"No. We'll just be taking notes."

Disappointment was written all over their fallen faces.

Wyatt asked the boys how old they were. They were both thirteen. He asked about their costumes, and their descriptions were similar to those given by Annika Johansson, confirming that these were the same boys.

"Now, tell me what you saw at the house on Hallowe'en night."

"We really liked all the animatronics and spooky sounds," the first boy said.

"We weren't that close to the house, though," the second boy explained.

"Not right away. We were behind a lady. I think she was the fairy's mother."

"The fairy was at the door talking to the man–"

"And there was a witch behind her. A tall one."

"Yeah. At first we thought he was an older teenager–"

"But when he went into the house, we figured he worked for the man and was dressed in costume. We thought it was kinda cool."

"Did this person have on a mask?"

"I don't know. His back was to us."

The second boy nodded.

"But you're saying 'he'. What makes you think it was a man?"

The boys looked at each other. "I don't know. Just because he was so tall," one said.

Wyatt nodded. It was interesting that they had pictured a man, whereas Mrs. Johansson had pictured a woman. It was the first time the idea of a tall male entered the equation. "So the fairy had left by then," Wyatt said.

"Yeah. She ran right by us."

"I heard her mother telling her they had to hurry."

"I saw her picture in the paper. I think her mother was hurrying her because she was in the costume competition."

"So it was the same girl?" Wyatt asked.

The boys nodded.

Wyatt nodded. "Okay, so the witch goes inside the house. What happened then?"

"We left."

"You left? Didn't you want to get candy from him?"

"No. We just came to see the light show."

"We wanted to get to the Community Centre. There was lots to do there."

"And candy, too, if we wanted it."

Wyatt glanced at Foxcroft. She shook her head imperceptibly.

"I want to thank you boys for coming in. You've been very helpful."

The parents looked proud. The boys beamed. They left.

"Well, what do you think of that, Foxcroft? Now we've got a tall male witch. That gives us something more to go on."

He found Ray and Jimmy conferring in the incident room. "You already interviewed the electrician, Jimmy?"

"Yes, and I learned some things that might have a bearing on the case."

"Fire away."

"It seems that five crew members worked on the display in one capacity or another. It so happened that that was the week when Nygaard was scouting locations. So no filming was going on. All five had access to the house. They had ample time to snoop around. The gaffer had been given the code to the security system. He swore he didn't give it to any of the others."

"Mm-hmm. Interesting," Wyatt mused. "Check their backgrounds and alibis and whittle them down."

"On it, Chief."

Twenty

Tuesday, November 4th

This time, Chief Wyatt was prepared. This time, the arrival of four mobile television units clogging up the street wouldn't faze him. This time a myriad of microphones stuck near his mouth wouldn't cause his blood to boil. This time he would keep his cool.

The large table in the conference room had been removed, leaving behind the twelve chairs. Wyatt figured that any more than that and there wouldn't be room for all the reporters who would be jostling for space.

Promptly at 2:30, he and Davidova walked through the connecting door from his office. Ray, Jimmy, McDaniel and Novak stood at the back of the room knowing it would be entertaining, if nothing else. Everyone quieted down as she stepped to the lectern and held up a letter-size piece of paper. "I'm Media Liaison, Marina Davidova. You should have one of these information sheets, so you'll know the spelling of my name. Other names and information are also listed here. Chief William Wyatt will now make a brief announcement, after which he will take questions." She stepped aside and Wyatt took her place.

He began by telling them who the victim was and when the body was discovered. "It appears to be a targeted killing. There were witnesses in the vicinity and they've come forward with information that we hope will lead to a suspect. As the investigation is in its early stages there's nothing further to report at this time."

The usual questions shot up like mushrooms.

How was he killed? "He was shot."

How many times? "We're not giving out that information."

Have you found the weapon? "No."

Who discovered the body? "A neighbour."

Who's the neighbour? "We're not giving out that information."

How come the neighbour saw the body? "He had a key from the rental agency."

Why was he there? "A crew member from *Paradise Pines* was banging on Nygaard's door. It roused his attention."

Why was the crew member there so early? "He'd been scheduled to pick up Mr. Nygaard for the day's shoot."

Who's the crew member? "We're not giving out that information."

Did he see the body? "As far as I know, only the neighbour saw it."

Do you have any leads? "We're pursuing every line of inquiry."

Any idea who did it? "No."

Any idea why he was murdered? "No."

Then the reporter from the French channel held up his hand–something that none of the others had done while peppering Wyatt with their questions. Wyatt pointed to the man.

"Jean-Luc LaRose from TVA1. Monsieur Nygaard had been arrested in two thousand nine for illegal drug use. Do you think his death could be drug related?"

The question caught Wyatt off guard. He hesitated. "We haven't received the toxicology report yet, so I can't answer that."

And LaRose caught Wyatt's pause. "But were there illegal drugs at the scene?"

"No."

When he said "Merci," it gave the other reporters the opening to return to their questioning.

He had a reputation for chasing women. Could it be someone's boyfriend or husband taking revenge on him? "He'd only been here two or so weeks. Seems too short a time for that. If it was someone from the past, why would he wait until Nygaard was in Canada?"

There don't seem to be any reporters here from the American media. "Well, that's a break for you because you're getting the scoop."

One of the reporters spoke out loud: "Some scoop. More like a teaspoon."

Wyatt's lips shaped into the semblance of a smile.

Is *Paradise Pines* going to close down production now? "No. It's my understanding that they've already got another director."

Who's that? "I don't know. Maybe your questions about the show should be addressed to them. That's everything for now." He stepped away from the lectern and Davidova thanked them for coming.

The reporters scrambled out of the room with their meagre notes and cellphones while others made live announcements from their mobile units. It should have been a sensational story. Not one of them was happy. Except Wyatt.

He walked straight back to the kitchen and poured himself a drink of water, not wanting to take what was available on the lectern. He thought it would make him look nervous. Marina followed him. They were joined by everyone else. "That was fun, wasn't it?" he said.

"There was only one question I found interesting," Jimmy said.

"Was it the one about drugs?" Wyatt asked.

"Yes."

"Trust it to be another French reporter," Ray said snidely.

"How did he know Nygaard was arrested if the charges were dropped?" McDaniel asked.

"Must read *The Hollywood Reporter*," Novak chuckled.

Wyatt turned to Atkins. "Where is Dr. D. with her tox report? Call her and find out when we're going to get it."

Atkins obliged him and returned within minutes telling them that no illegal drugs had been detected in his blood at the time of death, but that didn't mean he wasn't using because enzymes in blood cells continue to break drugs down after death–particularly cocaine. "She's sending over the preliminary report later today."

"So it may or may not be drug related. But because a weapon's involved, I think we should be exploring that possibility. God, I hope it isn't. I hate the thought of bringing in known dealers. Scum of the earth–after pedophiles. But they're the ones who carry."

"A low-life would hang on to his piece," Novak suggested. "And he would be smart enough to pick up the shell casings."

Jimmy had remained silent throughout the post-press conference scrum. Wyatt looked at him questioningly. "What's your take on this, Tan?"

"I'm thinking of the timeline here. Was Nygaard waiting for someone and viewing the dailies while he waited? A partially eaten pizza was beside the computer and a plate and open box of pizza were on the kitchen table. Was it someone who knew he would be alone watching dailies? If so, it would have to be someone from the company. Or you could be right. Perhaps a dealer came by, maybe to get some money, or for some other reason. Whatever, there was an altercation and Nygaard wound up with a lump on his head. Later on he was shot. So what happened in those intervening hours?"

"Jeez, Jimmy. You're giving me a headache," Ray said.

As promised, Dr. D. transmitted the report by mid-afternoon. "It's pretty straightforward," Atkins told Wyatt. "But one thing popped up."

"What's that?"

"The long black cotton thread that she removed from the deceased's neck. He wasn't wearing anything similar in colour or material. So it was an outside source, which may give us a lead. The lab report came back on the pills and kitchen items. Nothing sinister there. The vitamins and supplements were exactly that."

Wyatt waited for more, but Atkins closed the folder. "That's it?"

"That's it," Atkins told him.

"Well, something might turn up to explain that thread. Any indication when the full report is forthcoming?"

"She's waiting for Vancouver on the bullets.

"Okay. Thanks, Josh."

Wyatt puffed out an impatient breath. It was only day three, but he was already straining at the leash.

Twenty-one

G o fish!" Sara shouted gleefully. So far, she had her first book of four cards on the table. Delilah had none. As Delilah reached into the pond of scattered cards, Sara noticed that she wasn't wearing the ring she always wore. She liked that ring. Even though Delilah had told her the diamond was small, it seemed big when sunlight caught it.

"You don't have your ring on," she said.

"You're a very observant girl, Sara." The card she selected didn't match any in her hand. She tried not to scowl so as to tip off Sara. "I think I've either lost it, or misplaced it, and can't remember where I put it."

"A boy at school found a ring in his trick or treat bag."

Delilah looked up, hope in her eyes. "Really? I've been wondering if that's what happened. Maybe it slid off when I dropped in the candy."

"But he doesn't live around here. So it's probably not your ring."

"Oh, that's too bad. I said a prayer to Jesus asking Him to help me."

"Does Jesus answer your prayers?"

"Sometimes He does. Sometimes He doesn't. I guess He's just too busy with really big stuff." Then she thought about Scott. Wasn't that one of the biggest things there could be? A mother praying for her child? But maybe the Lord just wanted that sweet boy in heaven with all the other good people. This was not the first time that explanation had come to her, and it did give her some comfort.

At last, Sara asked for a card that Delilah did not have. "Go fish!" Delilah told her. The doorbell rang. "It's probably your mother," she said. "Why don't you go see."

Sara ran for the door, saw that it was her mother and before Annika got two feet inside the house, told her about the missing ring.

Annika turned to Delilah. "I saw a notice in the lost and found column in this morning's paper about someone finding a wedding ring. Maybe it's yours. Do you have the paper?"

"I do." She went to the basket on the floor beside her recliner. "I can't find my magnifying glass, so I haven't read it yet. Here it is." She handed *The Bayside Bugle* to Annika who read the ad. "Found: A gold wedding band with one diamond." Then she read out the phone number.

"Oh," Delilah said, disappointed. "It says one diamond. It doesn't say anything about the other two little ones on either side."

"Maybe because they don't want to give out too many details. Someone may say it's theirs, but if they don't mention that, then the person who found it knows they aren't the real owners."

"Oh, my. You can't trust anyone anymore."

"I'll call the number." She got out her cellphone. When a woman answered Annika handed the phone to her.

"What do I talk into? There's no speaker," she said agitated.

"Put it up to your ear like a regular phone and just talk," Annika said.

"Hello! Hello! Can you hear me?" Delilah shouted. Annika and Sara were starting to laugh. And Delilah heard laughter coming into her ear as well. And then a voice.

"Yes, I can hear you just fine. Can you hear me?"

Delilah was confounded by the clear sound coming from a slab of plastic. "Yes. I can hear you. Did you find a ring? My friend here tells me you found a wedding ring."

"Yes. Can you tell me when you lost it?"

"Not exactly, but it was around Hallowe'en. I can't remember the last time I saw it. But I'll tell you what it looks like." After giving a good description of the ring, the woman confirmed that it matched the ring she had. She got the address and said it would take a while to get there because they lived in the outskirts of the Township.

Delilah yelled, "Hallelujah! My prayers have been answered." She then began to tear up and reached for a tissue in her apron pocket.

"Oh, Delilah, don't cry," Sara said.

"These are tears of joy, darling."

"It's nice that Jesus answered your prayers."

Annika frowned. She worried about Sara expecting prayers to be answered, and determined to have a chat with her about that.

It wasn't long before the woman arrived with the ring. She explained that it had been in her son's trick or treat bag.

"Well, I'll be jiggered," Delilah said, amazed. "I guess it just slipped off my bony fingers when I was putting a treat inside his bag."

"It looks that way," the woman agreed. "We always come to the village for Hallowe'en because the streets are flat and the houses are close together."

"I was very lucky this time. I guess I'll have to keep my eye on it from now on." Delilah wanted to give her a reward, but the woman would have none of it. She was just glad to be able to return it.

After they left, Annika said it was time for them to go, too. "Thanks for keeping Sara company, Delilah. It took me a long time to get my shopping done because I had to keep driving around the parking lot until I got a spot. Television trucks took up all the spots on the street by the police station. And the aisles inside Bayside Foods were jammed because of their dollar forty-nine day specials. Sara would have been run over."

"No, I wouldn't. You just don't like me to go shopping with you. You think I *dawdle!*" She had heard the word more than once.

The women laughed because it was true. With her curiosity about everything, she was a distraction to Annika, who just wanted to get in and out as quickly as possible.

Delilah hated to bother Ariel again, but it was late afternoon already and she hoped to get the letter into *Brickbats and Bouquets* before the paper came out on Thursday. An aroma reminiscent of her childhood filled her nostrils when Ariel opened the door. *Yep. Ham hocks and cabbage.* "Hi Ariel. I'm sorry to bother you, but I need you to write another letter to the paper."

"It's no trouble at all, Lilah. Come on in."

"Something smells good."

"It's a very thick French soup called garbure. The base is ham hock. I'm just about to add the Savoy cabbage to it."

"I've seen that kind of cabbage in the grocery store, but I've never bought it. Just get the ordinary *kapusta*."

Ariel added the cabbage then got her pen and piece of paper.

Delilah held out her left hand. "Take a gander at this."

"Oh! You've got your ring back! Who returned it?"

So Delilah told her the story of how she lost it.

"I didn't see that ad in the paper. I don't usually read them," Ariel said. "Perhaps I should."

"I'm just thankful Annika did. So I want people to know that it was found and put the lady's name in the paper. It's the least I could do. She wouldn't take any reward money."

"That's a nice thing to do. Let's work on the wording." They got their heads together and came up with something that pleased Delilah.

"I'll take it down right now," she said.

"You don't need to do that. We'll phone it in this time," Ariel said. She looked up the number, called the paper and read the copy. "And you're sure it will get into Thursday's paper? ... Thank you very much." She turned to Delilah. "They'll get it in."

"That's a relief."

"Why don't you stay for dinner? It will be early because I have choir practice."

"That's fine with me. I like to eat early. I'll go home and feed Tabitha first, and put on my best bib and tucker."

Ariel was sure it meant that she wouldn't be wearing her apron over her muumuu and long johns.

Twenty-two

Jade and Percy sat side-by-side at the kitchen table leafing through the picture album of herself and Blythe when they were teenagers. Plates with the remains of apple pie had been shoved aside.

"The first time I stepped into this house, I knew what a real home was supposed to be like," she said. "It was everything ours wasn't. So warm and lived in. I envied Blythe. And I couldn't believe she chose me to be her friend. Me. Bucktooth and shy."

"We weren't surprised, Jade. She told us about the ragging you took from your classmates. It was just like her to take you under her wing. And she got a lot out of your friendship, you know. She admired you. Thought you were brave and brilliant."

Jade laughed. "My brains are what kept me sane ... and safe. If I had been stupid, can you imagine how much worse it would've been for me?"

Percy studied her. "Jade, can you tell me more about why Blythe ran off? I was out fishing every summer and it would've been the best time to talk to her–while she was out of school on holiday. But I couldn't. And my sister was busy with her job. So she wasn't there for her much, either."

Jade didn't want to tell him all of it. It was unnecessary and would cause him more grief. But she gave him the Coles Notes version. "Well, she was completely shattered when Jeannie died. It did a number on her head. It was all I could do to keep her from quitting school and missing out on her graduation. But I knew her plan was to move away. She dreamed of going to Vancouver to take a modelling course she had read about. That's why she took a job at the drug store–to earn some money." She looked at Percy. "Are you sure you want to hear what happened?"

He took in a long breath, let it out slowly and nodded.

"Right after high school, she saw an ad in *The Vancouver Sun*–those were the days before you could place an ad on line–and moved into an apartment with a couple of other girls. She got a job at the same drug store chain and then went for an interview at a modelling agency. But they told her she would never be a clothing model because her breasts were too big. But with her looks, she could be a photographer's model. They could train her for that. It was during one of the shoots that a photographer asked her if she would like her picture sent to *Playboy* magazine. She was shocked. Told him she could never pose nude. What he did do without telling her was send some pictures to a friend in Los Angeles, who showed them to Berens Nygaard. And I think you know the rest, Percy."

"Yeah, that bastard used her and when he got tired of her, he passed her off to someone else."

"The thing is, she never fell out of love with Berens, and Danny Klebach knew that. That's why he killed her … and himself."

Percy ran a hand over one of the pictures. "She was so beautiful. And I didn't have time for her."

Jade held his hand. His fingers squeezed hers so hard it took all of her will power not to pull away from the pain. She knew he was trying to control his emotions. "When I heard that Nygaard was here, I was afraid for him. I believed you would kill him if you ever got the chance."

His face turned white.

"The police came to see me. It seems the killer was wearing a witch's costume that smelled of patchouli." She paused before continuing, watching his reaction. "And Sara Johansson smelled it. She thought it was me. Luckily I have a good alibi." She paused. "Do you still have that costume?"

He shook his head.

"I hope you don't have any patchouli oil."

"Just a tiny vial."

"Then give it to me. It might arouse suspicions if the police ever happen to find it here."

He got up shakily, left the room and returned shortly. When he handed it to her, she gave him a long hug. "I guess we'll be going to our graves with this secret," she said.

"I'm sorry, Jade."

"My life is full of secrets, Percy. One more can't cause me any more grief than I've already known." But she doubted that was the truth.

Jimmy arrived home to find the table set and Delilah sitting with Roger on her lap. "This is a nice picture," he said, removing his jacket and hanging it in the entryway closet. "I see you have a new friend."

"His hair feels like silk," Delilah said.

"It's the cod," Ariel said. "We buy fresh filets, cut them into small pieces and freeze them, then boil them at feeding time. It's much better than canned food." She was dragging a wooden spoon through the Dutch oven as she spoke. Then she left it standing in the middle of the soup. "Look at this," she said, laughing. "The recipe said you should be able to do this if it's done right."

"So is this the first time you've made it? Are we're going to be guinea pigs?" Delilah asked.

"No. I've already tasted it and it's delicious." She got out a baguette, sliced it and put it on the table along with butter. "This is how the French eat it, so tonight we'll all be French."

She ladled the soup into big bowls and they began to eat. After a few minutes—and the occasional "mmms" from Delilah—Jimmy got up, opened the fridge, took out a can of beer and poured it into a glass.

"Beer?" Ariel asked with accusation in her voice.

He shrugged. "The soup is salty."

"It's not salty. It's savoury." Her chin rose. "There's a difference."

"That differentiation is lost on me. It tastes salty."

"Well, you're not eating the bread, Jimmy. You're supposed to eat bread with this soup," she huffed.

Delilah nodded. "You know, bread and salt go together. A Russian friend of mine told me that bread and salt are offered as wedding presents."

Ariel smiled. She had an advocate. "So, eat your bread, Jimmy."

"Okay." He took a piece of the baguette, added butter and began to eat it. Then he had some soup. "You're right. It's much less salty now." He smiled. "Dare I say savoury?"

The women laughed.

After the dishes had been cleared away, they sat and discussed the case, Jimmy sharing some of the details. It was becoming something of a routine for them … unfortunate as that might be. The only one missing was Lana, but she had other interests these days.

"Something came up at the press conference today that we may pursue. Because right now we have nothing except for the fact that a witch smelling of patchouli went into the house just after six o'clock."

"A lot of hippies still use that godawful stuff," Delilah said. "Some of them live in a section of the Township. When they come into town for the Thursday night street market or the farmer's market on Saturday mornings, you can smell it on them."

"How do you know about patchouli, Lilah?" Ariel asked, as she took a sip of the white Bordeaux.

"I was in my twenties when the so-called summer of love arrived. We used to douse ourselves in it. That's where I met Melvin—at a love-in."

Ariel nearly choked on her wine. "You're just full of surprises, Lilah."

"You can't reach my age and not have a few tucked up your sleeve," she cackled. "What were you were saying about the press conference, Jimmy?"

"A reporter asked if the murder might be drug related because Nygaard had been a known user."

"Was he still using?" Delilah asked.

"There was no evidence of it."

"Was he ever arrested for it?" Ariel asked.

"Yes. In two thousand nine, according to the French-Canadian reporter."

"You think he stiffed a dealer and maybe that's who offed him?" Delilah wondered.

Ariel and Jimmy burst into laughter. No matter how many times she used gangster speak, it still sounded funny coming from her.

"It's possible, but unlikely. And something else. Nygaard had some strange things among his vitamins … turmeric and ginkgo biloba."

"Aha! That would go along with what you were saying about the list he kept of crew members' names."

"What do you mean?" Jimmy asked.

"What's that stuff?" Delilah asked.

"He probably thought he was losing his memory." Ariel responded. "Gingko biloba is purported to help with that, but studies have shown that it doesn't."

"What about turmeric?"

"Well, that's an altogether different kettle of fish. It apparently does help with memory and overall brain function."

Jimmy and Delilah laughed.

"You sound like a commercial," he said.

"More like Helmut at the health food store," Delilah said. "But if it helps, maybe I should get some. It seems like I'm forgetting more and more things every day."

"We all are," Ariel said, attempting to placate her neighbour.

"According to a couple of people, Nygaard was showing signs of memory loss. And he was irritable, and suspicious to the point of paranoia. Sounds like dementia, doesn't it?"

"Sort of," Ariel agreed.

"How was he killed?"

"Can't tell you that right now, Delilah."

"I know, but my intuition is telling me he was shot. After all, drugs and guns go together."

"Then I'll have to be extra careful what I say around you from now on."

"That would be no fun. But I'll keep my opinion to myself, if anyone should ask."

"Thank you."

That sealed it for her. She knew she had been right. "It's time to go. I have a date with another Jimmy," she added, with a grin.

"And who might that be?" Ariel asked.

"Detective Inspector Jimmy Perez. But he's in Scotland."

"Then you'd better hurry. They're eight hours ahead of us."

Twenty-three

Wednesday, November 5th

Percy hadn't slept. His conversation with Jade had not made him feel better–but worse. It didn't matter that he and Jade had a secret. He couldn't live with it anymore. The weight of it was too much. He decided to confess. As soon as the idea entered his mind, he felt lighter. He surveyed his house. The police would probably search it. No sense in leaving it looking a mess. He washed all the dishes, threw out old food, cleaned the toilet and sink, swept the floors and made the bed. Then he showered and shaved, took out his cleanest shirt and only suit and got dressed. It was just past noon.

When the elderly man stepped up to the reception desk, Mary Beth smiled and wondered what he was doing there. "Can I help you?"

"Yes, I'd like to speak to Chief Wyatt about the murder of Berens Nygaard," he said quietly.

Thinking he might be another witness, she asked for his name, wrote it down and said she would let the chief know. She got up and knocked on Wyatt's opened door.

"What is it, Mary Beth?"

"I think a witness just walked in."

After taking the proffered note and listening to her description, he thought the same thing. "I'll be out in a second," he told her. He walked over to Ray and Jimmy and spoke softly. "We may have another witness. He's at reception. I'll talk to him in my office. You go in. Take notes."

Wyatt walked to the front and saw a weather-worn but nicely dressed senior in the lobby. "Good afternoon, Mr. Goodbody. I'm Chief William Wyatt. Won't you come this way, please?"

The man said nothing as he followed Wyatt into his office. He was taken aback to see two officers already seated in the room. They got up when he entered. Wyatt made introductions, then offered him a chair.

"I understand you may be a witness to the events surrounding the death of Mr. Nygaard," he began very formally.

"No ... no, I'm not a witness. I killed him!"

"Mr. Goodbody, I am advising you once again to retain a lawyer," Wyatt said, after moving to an interview room. "This is a very serious matter and you need legal counsel before you make any statements."

Percy regarded him with his red-rimmed, watery blue eyes. "What would he do except charge me money? I know I'm guilty. So what's the point?"

"If that's your wish, then perhaps we'll start. This interview will be videotaped and recorded."

Percy said he had no problem with that.

Wyatt then got busy with the preamble and the fact that Goodbody had confessed to the crime. "First of all, why do you think you are guilty of Mr. Nygaard's death?"

He relayed the details of how he had entered the home, how Nygaard had enraged him by a comment he made, and how he pushed him, causing him to fall, hitting his head, and dying.

In the observation room, the partners shook their heads. "I knew it was too good to be true," Ray said. "Wyatt's gonna want to know why he did that, though."

"Before we go any further, Mr. Goodbody, I want you to know that you did not kill Mr. Nygaard. He revived after you left."

Percy's mouth gaped open. "But I don't understand. He had no pulse," he argued.

"How do you know that?"

"Because I took it," he sputtered.

It was at that moment that Wyatt realized the significance of the long black thread.

"Mr. Goodbody, were you wearing a witch's costume, by any chance?"

Percy was taken aback briefly, then smiled sadly. "Oh, someone saw me after all."

Wyatt did not confirm that. "Did you perhaps have on black gloves when you took his pulse?"

Percy's eyes flew open. *How did they know this?* "Yes, I did."

"Perhaps that's why you didn't feel his pulse. He had only been knocked unconscious when he fell. His pulse might have been weak or even stopped briefly. It's been known to happen. But he was not dead. He came to. Someone else killed him."

"How do you know that?" He was becoming belligerent.

"Because he died of gunshot wounds."

Percy's shock knocked him back in his chair. "Shot? Someone came after me and shot him?"

"That's what I'm saying."

"But I was so sure he was dead."

"It's not the first time people have made this mistake."

He sighed in relief.

Ray whispered to Jimmy: "Kewpie had a corpse wake up. Scared the bejesus out of him. I heard that's when he lost his hair."

Wyatt proved Ray's earlier words to be correct. He wanted to know why Goodbody had gone to see Nygaard.

"It doesn't matter now, since I'm not the person who killed him. It was an accident."

"But you fled the scene, Mr. Goodbody. In legal terms, that is *mens rea*—a criminal intention or knowledge that an act is wrong. So before we go any further, you need to answer that question." Wyatt waited while the man weighed what to say. "Mr. Goodbody, do you have a reason why you don't want to tell us?"

"I just don't want to dig up the past." He paused, lifted both hands. and let out a long ragged breath. "Of course, it would've all come out anyway if I had killed the bastard." He took a deep breath. "Does the name Blythe O'Neill mean anything to you?"

Prickles picked up the hairs on Wyatt's arms. "Yes, it does," he said quietly.

"That was my daughter."

"*Madonn'!*" Ray blurted out.

"What?"

"I'll tell you later," he said. "I gotta hear this."

Wyatt cleared his throat. "I'm so sorry, Mr. Goodbody."

"So you see, I had a very good reason to want him dead. But really, all I wanted was him gone. Out of Britannia Bay." He paused and gently added, "out of Blythe's home."

"But it wasn't Nygaard who killed your daughter. It was someone else," Wyatt reminded him.

"Yes, but *that* man was someone Nygaard pushed on Blythe because he got tired of her. So, in a way, he did kill her."

"Well, it seems that Nygaard has raised the wrath of someone else. So whoever it was spared you jail time … or anymore publicity."

Percy nodded. "It's been a horrible week, I can tell you."

"I can imagine. I appreciate the fact that you came in to confess, even though you're not culpable. I'm going to overlook the fact that you left someone for dead. So you're free to go." Wyatt ended the recording and stood up. "By the way, what did you do with the witch's costume?"

"I shredded it. So you see, I was planning on *not* confessing and taking my secret to the grave."

"It would've been hard to live with."

"Just living is hard. You don't get to choose what life throws at you. Or when."

Afterwards, Ray told Jimmy the story of Blythe O'Neill. "He carried around that pain and anger all those years," he concluded.

"There's no statute of limitations on revenge."

Percy rushed home and picked up the phone. "Jade. I didn't kill him!"

"What do you mean?"

"Someone else killed him. He was shot!"

"How do you know that?"

"I went in to confess—"

"You did what!?"

"I couldn't stand the guilt, Jade. It just wasn't me. I've always been honest. It was eating away at me. I had to do it and accept the consequences."

"Oh, Percy. You're just too good for your own good."

"That makes two of us."

And now that we know you're innocent of the murder, how do you feel?" Jade asked a relaxed Percy.

"Like a great weight has been lifted off me, Jade. For years I wanted him dead, so I'm glad someone else did, too, and carried it out."

"Perhaps it was someone in the production company. Someone with a grudge."

"Perhaps."

"You're being very coy, here, Percy. What's going on with you?"

"Well, in fact, I had been wondering if it was you."

"Me?"

"Yes. You know … because Blythe was like a sister to you. So you had a reason to kill him, too."

"That's true, Percy. But I didn't even know where he lived."

He was struck with that realization. "Oh, of course. You would have had no way of knowing that."

"I'm pretty much a hermit. My world consists of the farms around here where I get most of my food and things for my chickens. My trips to town are minimal and brief. I never read newspapers. So how would I know anything about this television show? *You* were the one who told me Nygaard was here."

"That's right. Me and my big mouth." And they laughed together for the first time in a long time. He wanted to cry.

Twenty-four

Henry Harlow stepped off the Twin Otter aircraft and thought he had landed in Smalltown, USA, but set in paradise. The flight over from Vancouver had been spectacular. He now understood why so many famous actors flew up to this part of Canada to do some sport fishing.

The pilot unloaded the baggage himself, and pointed the way to the terminal–a small, single-storey gray and white building with no redeeming architectural features.

Harlow scanned the skyline. He could see nothing but trees. Picking up his compact bag, he walked into the terminal. What he needed was a rental car. Was that even possible? He mentally berated himself for not checking before leaving Los Angeles. Then he spotted a sign. "Fleet Street. Car Rentals." *Well, looky here. Probably a fleet of one car.*

At the counter, a young man was playing a game on his cellphone. Quickly standing up, he put the device away. "Good afternoon, sir. Are you wanting to rent a car?"

"I am."

As the young man started his spiel about rates and insurance coverage, Harlow held up his hand. "I have rented many a car in my lifetime, so I know the drill and I accept the liabilities, and so on. So if it's all right with you, we can skip that and proceed with the paperwork. Here is my credit card."

When he held it out, the young man frowned. "I'm sorry, sir. We don't take that card here."

"You don't? Why not?"

He shrugged. "Something to do with the fees they charge companies. You won't find a restaurant or motel or B&B around here who will accept it."

Harlow slotted away the card. "Guess I can leave home without it after all," he said.

The young man chuckled. "Do you have another card?"

He fished out a second card and handed it over.

"This is perfect. Thanks." When he read the corporate name on the card, he realized why the man had come to Britannia Bay.

In the parking lot, Harlow sat in the driver's seat of a late-model sedan with a GPS. "I'll need the address of the police station."

"No, you won't," the clerk confidently told him, giving him explicit directions.

"What about the local newspaper office?"

"That's *The Bayside Bugle*. It's down the same street on the next corner. That's Church Street. You can't miss it."

Famous last words, Harlow thought. "What about the directions for Charterhouse B&B?"

A wry smile creased the young man's face. "Oh. You're staying with the Abernathys, eh? That's worth a story itself." He gave him the address. "By the way, are you familiar with roundabouts?"

"A little." He wasn't going to mention driving in London during his university days, dashing in and out of the lanes with his heart in his mouth hoping everyone was on the same page.

The clerk then proceeded to give him the rules and what to watch out for.

Harlow listened patiently. "It sounds complicated. But I'll be careful," he said soberly. No flies on that young man, he thought, driving off. *But what's with the Abernathys?*

At the station, Ray and Jimmy were examining everything they had learned so far, which was a paltry amount. "What about interviewing the driver again?" Jimmy suggested. "He spent time taking Nygaard from point A to point B. They might have had some chats. Or maybe

Arellano overhead something in a phone call. Who knows? I just think we gave him a pass after he found the body."

"And a Hail Mary during his formal interview," Ray nodded. "I'm up for that."

Arellano was surprised he had been called back. "This is the third time I've talked to you guys. I don't think I have anything else to tell you."

"This is nothing to do with the morning of the murder, or your alibi. This has to do with you being Nygaard's driver," Ray told him.

"Oh. Okay."

"Did you talk to him about anything other than the show?"

"We didn't talk about anything. Period. He sat in the back. He was always talking to himself. I couldn't hear him but I guessed he was repeating lines from the script. He always had a copy with him."

"Can you tell us anything about his habits when he was off the set?"

It took Arellano a few minutes of thinking. Then he grinned. "He did this funny thing every time we got to the house. He would check all his pockets, sometimes more than twice."

"What did you think he was doing?"

"Searching for the key."

"Did you ever drive him out of Britannia Bay for any reason?"

"No."

"What about picking up packages for him?"

"No."

"Did anyone else ask you to drive them out of the area?"

"No."

"Or run errands for them?"

He was about to answer in the negative again when he stopped. "Um ... the only time was a trip to the ferry terminal one day with the Assistant Props Master."

"The ferry terminal?"

"Yeah. There was a package arriving from Vancouver that he was told to pick up."

"What did he do?"

"He went into the waiting room and came right out carrying a box."

"How big a box?"

He gave dimensions with his hands. "About eighteen by eighteen inches."

"Did he open it?"

"Yes."

"What was in it?" Both Ray and Jimmy were holding their breaths.

"A wig."

"A wig?"

"Yes, Miss Blair needed a new wig because the one she was using was causing her head to itch. She was allergic to something in it. So we had to get right back to the set."

The buildup and letdown caused both Ray and Jimmy to laugh. Arellano joined in, then asked what was so funny.

"It's a long story, Mr. Arellano. Thanks very much for coming in."

"You're welcome." He left, still wondering what the joke was.

Twenty-five

The Abernathys had received the reservation with a mixture of awe and anxiety. "We knew foreign reporters would be coming, Daphne, especially from Hollywood. At least he's not from some sleazy tabloid."

"Do you think he will be asking us for information?"

"Oh, *indubitably*. But we have *nothing* to tell him, do we?"

"Well, Nygaard *did* stay here for four nights," she reminded her husband.

"But there was absolutely *nothing* unusual about his sojourn."

"But Clive—" she began in whispered words.

"Hush, Daphne," he interrupted her just as quietly. "We don't want to get *involved*. We don't want the police *swarming* here searching the place. Turning over *everything* in his room. Just think about the *upheaval* if that were to happen. No. If we are asked, we won't say anything. It will be our position that Mr. Nygaard only slept and ate breakfast here. That after his arrival, we didn't see him to talk to him. He left after breakfast and came in late, and when he checked out, he simply put his key on the front desk. At least *that's* all true."

Daphne kept biting her lips and massaging her hands. "If you say so, dear. But my book club is already tittering about it. They want all the gossip, of course."

"Well, this time you *must* stay silent. Don't even *hint* at anything untoward. Do you understand, Daphne?"

"But what about Louise? After all it was her who found—"

"Daphne," he drilled his eyes into hers. "What did I just say?"

She lowered her head.

"I'll repeat the same thing to Louise. She won't say a word if she wants to keep her job. By the way, do you still have it tucked away somewhere?"

She nodded.

"I think you should discard it. Otherwise it will be a constant reminder. Now, I'm sorry if it sounds like I'm badgering you, pet, but this is *très important*. Now, let's have a cup of tea and wait for our American guest."

Their American guest was currently sitting with Keith Kittridge, with whom he had been chatting for a quarter of an hour or so. "I was a cub reporter in a newsroom much like this one, Keith. It even smells the same. Brings back a lot of great memories, I can tell you." Having arrived with preconceived ideas, he was relieved to be able to ignore them. He found the local newspaper editor friendly and cooperative, and informed. After reading the newspaper report, he was surprised that this seemingly mellow fellow had gone for the jugular, not holding back on Nygaard's past proclivities.

"It's not much different from my early days. I seem to have found a niche and turned it into a trench," Keith said, wryly.

"I'm assuming you get enough ad revenue to keep putting out a paper. It's not easy these days."

"Just barely. It keeps me awake nights, I can tell you. The one good thing is the demographics of the area. A lot of older folks are used to reading a paper. And we get a lot of support from local businesses. But it would be nice to have more. We operate on the proverbial shoestring."

Harlow nodded his head as he took another sip of the coffee. He needed something to eat, and soon, or his blood sugar levels would dip dangerously low. He tapped the copy of the paper. "This police chief must be a terrific poker player."

Kittridge smiled. "Wyatt the wily. Says nothing with even fewer words. In fact, there's not much more to write up right now. But if I know the boys at the station, they'll keep digging until they find something."

Harlow got up. "Thanks for your time, Keith. But I'm starving. Can you tell me where I can grab something to eat?"

Knowing Justine's had closed, he began listing the few available choices. When he said "El Coyote," Harlow stopped him.

"Mexican? Really? Here?"

"And it's damn good," Kittridge said. "It's four doors away, up Hill Street."

"Well, Mexican is like home cooking for me. So I'll give them a try."

"Tell them I sent you. And they may give you the *real* salsa. Not the stuff they give to people who think bottled chili sauce should come with a warning label."

"Thank you very much for seeing me. I appreciate it–from one new-shound to another."

"Drop in anytime." After Harlow left, Kittridge picked up the reporter's business card. He looked at what he had written on the back. "Hank the Hack." He laughed. The man didn't take himself too seriously, a trait he admired.

Twenty-six

Harlow had taken Kittridge's advice, told Miguel Flores that Kittridge had sent him, and the special salsa was placed on the table. "*Es muy picante*," Miguel warned him.

"*Bien. Asi me gusta.*" After giving his order, he told them about another El Coyote restaurant located in Los Angeles where he spent a lot of evenings. Speaking Mexican Spanish the entire time, he had delighted Miguel and Teresa, who couldn't do enough for him. He was now well fed and well informed about what it was like for two ex-pats from Tampico to live among ex-pats from Britain. When he mentioned that he was here to cover the murder of Berens Nygaard, their faces drooped.

"Is lamentable to have so bad a thing to happen in this beautiful village," Miguel *tsked* and shook his head.

"Is three times in two years. Is very bad." Teresa's sorrowful eyes fell on Harlow. "We came here to escape violence."

"But it's not as bad as in most places, you have to admit," Harlow said.

"That is true. Especially Mexico. Now it is a country of war between the drug cartels. No one is safe. We are happy to be here."

"What are the police like here?"

They both smiled. "They are very nice. Very polite. They give us much business," Teresa said.

"I wonder if it's too late to drop in for a visit."

Miguel shook his head. "No. Chief Wyatt goes home every day at five-thirty."

Curious, Harlow asked him how he knew this.

"I know his car. I see him through my window." He grinned.

"You would make a good spy."

By now, all three were chuckling. Harlow made a final swipe of his mouth with the napkin. "I think I'll chance a visit with him—if he will see me, that is." He put down a U.S. twenty dollar bill, which Miguel picked up and handed back.

"No, no. Today you are our guest."

Teresa wagged a finger at him. "Tomorrow you pay."

Their laughter followed him out the door.

Ray, Jimmy and Wyatt were regarding the almost bare white board when Mary Beth came into the room. "Chief, a reporter is here from the *Los Angeles Herald*," she whispered.

"You're kidding me."

"No. I'm not. He's in the foyer. Here's his card."

Ray and Jimmy stood on either side of Wyatt as he read the card. "Well, I'll be damned."

"This could be a break," Ray said.

"I hope so. Let's go welcome the man," Wyatt said, and together they walked to the front. Every eye in the room followed, wondering what was going on.

"Mr. Harlow, I'm Chief William Wyatt, and these gentlemen are Detective Sergeants Ray Rossini and Jimmy Tan."

"Nice to meet you," he said, holding out his hand. That Wyatt accepted it almost bowled him over.

"Come on back to my office."

Harlow raised his eyebrows. "Really?"

"You're a visitor. We treat visitors well in this town," Wyatt said. Mary Beth, standing behind Harlow, flicked her eyes to the ceiling.

"Well, I won't lie. It's not often cops are willing to talk to the press," he said.

"Don't get me wrong. We're accommodating for a reason. It so happens that we need to pick your brain," Wyatt told him.

"Ah. I thought there had to be an ulterior motive." Harlow smiled.

As they walked to the back, squad members sized up their visitor. Medium height, lean, about fifty years old, tanned face, straight nose, moderate moustache, and light brown hair continuing down past his ears and circling his chin in a trim cut beard. His rugged jacket straight out of L.L. Bean, khaki pants and penny loafers screamed "American!" They made a bet—with no takers—that he had on a checked shirt underneath.

"Would you like a coffee? We've got an instant brew machine."

"No thanks. I just had a late lunch—or early dinner—and coffee at El Coyote."

"The Flores are fine folks," Wyatt said. "Great food, too."

They entered Wyatt's office and closed the door.

"Mind if I take off my coat? It's warm in here."

"No, make yourself comfortable," Wyatt said.

Harlow removed his jacket, revealing a checked shirt.

"Did you fly in?" Ray asked.

"Yes. The view was stunning."

Knowing the airline's schedule he surmised that Harlow had already been in town for a couple of hours. "Did you find a place to stay as well as eat?"

"Yes, I have a reservation at Charterhouse."

The three officers smiled. Harlow caught it. "There must be something about that place. The young fellow at the airport thought I would have story enough just staying with them."

"Let's just say you don't have to watch old British comedies if you spend any time around them."

"Well, at this point, I'm intrigued." He cleared his throat. "So, let's get down to scratching each other's backs. What do you want to know from me?"

"As you know from the press release, we are early days in this investigation, and don't have much to go on, except for some tension between Allen Benson and Berens Nygaard."

"That's understandable, considering their relationship."

Aw, hell. I hope they aren't lovers, Ray thought.

'What sort of relationship are we talking about here?" Wyatt asked.

"Benson is, or was, Nygaard's brother-in-law."

Jaws dropped in tandem. Then Wyatt spoke with muted anger. "Why hasn't anyone mentioned this? Particularly Benson himself? They've had plenty of opportunity to do that."

"Well, if you didn't know that, then you aren't going to know the rest of the riddle. First of all, do you know who Nygaard's wife is?"

Was another shoe about to drop?

Wyatt shook his head. "No."

"Her name is Bibi Benson."

"As in Allen Benson?" Ray asked.

"As in the actress?" Jimmy asked.

"Right on both counts," Harlow affirmed.

Wyatt looked at Jimmy. "She's famous?"

"Quite," Jimmy replied. He knew Wyatt didn't watch anything except old films, so he wouldn't have a clue about Bibi Benson.

"And there's more," Harlow continued. "Nygaard was arrested two years ago for assaulting Bibi Benson."

"What a can of worms." Ray threw up his hands.

"If I were Benson, I'd wring that guy's neck," Wyatt said.

"Might be a motive for a murder," Ray said.

Jimmy shook his head. "Too much time has passed. And too obvious."

"So what about this assault?" Wyatt asked.

"She caught him *in flagrante delicto* at the Bel Air Hotel with a starlet, someone Bibi had met on a set and befriended, which made it even more humiliating. Apparently Nygaard punched his wife and she wound up in the hallway outside his room, flat on her back with a black eye. All the shouting and screaming brought the hotel staff and someone took a picture. This time Nygaard couldn't say he didn't do it."

"What do you mean by 'this time'?" Ray asked.

"It wasn't the first time, but this time someone tipped her off."

"Probably the guy who took the picture."

"It seems she had sent out feelers to a few of the hotels that if they saw him with some pretty young thing to call her. He was notorious.

Why she stayed with him was beyond me. She could have had the pick of just about anyone. She's quite a beauty."

"Could she have stayed for monetary reasons?" Ray asked.

"Maybe. They have a mega mansion in Bel-Air and all the expenses that go with it. Plus, she shells out big bucks for cosmetic surgery, jewelry, cars–the whole nine yards. She can't live this lifestyle on her own even though she has had a pretty substantial career."

"What happened to the charges, or did she lay any?" Wyatt asked.

"No, she didn't, but all the publicity was probably sweet enough for her."

"Is that why he was *persona non grata* for a while, and no one was hiring him," Jimmy said.

"That and the arrest for drugs."

"Yeah, Benson mentioned that, but not the assault," Ray said.

"So with his death, she'll probably have to change her lifestyle," Ray added.

Harlow waited a moment before replying. "Not if she has a man of means waiting in the wings."

The conversation stalled as the officers absorbed this morsel of news. "Is that conjecture or fact?" Wyatt asked.

"She's pretty careful. At the moment, it's just idle gossip. But rumours are flying about a man who's been popping up in pictures with her and her group of friends. Now, all eyes are going to be on her. If there *is* anything going on between them, it will have to be put on ice until a decent interval passes."

"Who's the guy?" Ray asked.

"The buzz is that it's Avi Rothman."

"Who's he when he's home?" Wyatt asked.

"As it happens, he's the Executive Producer of *Paradise Pines*."

"Oooh, this is getting better and better," Ray said.

"I imagine Nygaard knew about it," Jimmy said.

"He might've."

"Well, it would be a convenient way for Rothman to get Nygaard out of town. Give him a job and leave the playing field to himself," Ray said.

"Now, I've given you some things to consider, so what can you give me to print?"

Wyatt shook his head. "I'm sorry to say that what we've got right now is nothing. Even after interviewing everyone, all we have are hypotheses. We're looking at a possible drug angle, even though no illegal drugs were found in his house or on his person."

"Of course that doesn't mean he hadn't been using."

"That's true."

"In the press release you said he was shot."

"That's right."

"Have you found the weapon?

"No."

"I know that drugs and guns are rampant in Vancouver," Harlow said.

"And they've spilled over here as well," Ray said. "It's led to more and more shootings."

"Yet you have some of the most stringent gun laws around."

"Doesn't mean the criminals won't get them," Wyatt said. "They can be smuggled in using creative methods."

"What's happening now is 3D printers that can make guns, or create parts that can turn some firearms into automatic weapons," Jimmy added. "We've got what we call 'ghost guns' floating around."

"You've got those, too?" Harlow said, amazed.

"Yep. Mom and Pop shops manufacturing and distributing untraceable firearms by using unregulated parts. And without serial numbers," Wyatt said.

"Sounds like you're a mini L.A.," Harlow said.

They nodded.

"So the gun has you thinking of a drugs angle, is that correct?"

"Right now, yes. But really, we're trying to catch straws in a windstorm. We may have to re-interview every person involved with the production."

"No one suddenly leave?"

"Not according to the Miss Brotman," Wyatt said. "Everyone is still here."

"Who is Miss Brotman?"

"Peggy Brotman. She's the Assistant to the Producer," Wyatt said.

"It would have been too blatant if someone left. He or she would be suspect number one," Jimmy said.

"If it turns out to be a drug hit after all, that person will be in the wind," Ray added.

"Seem to be a few wind metaphors going on here," Harlow snickered.

"Stick around. You'll find out why," Wyatt laughed.

"By the way, Teresa Flores mentioned that this is the third murder in a couple of years. What about the other two?"

Wyatt briefly recounted the first incident, then said, "Did you say you had talked to Keith Kittridge?"

"That's right."

"It so happens that last spring, one of his reporters was found dead. Might have been unintended consequences of a robbery. But it remains a cold case at the moment."

"So is the charm and beauty of this town just camouflage?" he smiled.

"No place is without its underlying dark side," Jimmy said.

Harlow agreed. "Well, I don't have much to file, but I'll send some copy down to L.A. tonight. Tell me what I can't use."

So Wyatt told him. Harlow grimaced. "Well I'll cobble together something. Have other American reporters shown up yet?"

"Not yet."

"Probably because they can't find you," Harlow said, laughing.

Twenty-seven

"So, what did we learn from his visit?" Wyatt asked his lead investigators.

"We learned that Nygaard's wife had a good reason to kill him, or have him killed," Jimmy said.

"Georgina's always saying she could murder me."

"I can understand that," Jimmy said.

"But that's all in fun. This is deadly serious," Wyatt said.

"Or just plain deadly. Let's look at Benson. He must have a lot of anger built up around the treatment of his sister," Jimmy said.

"It burns me that he never mentioned Nygaard was his brother-in-law or that his sister was a famous actress," Ray said.

"No. And those are damn good reasons to bring him in again." Wyatt slapped his palms on his desk. "Right. Get on the blower and tell him to come in tomorrow morning. We can't do much more today."

"One other thing, Chief," Jimmy said. "Peggy Brotman said she knew Benson pretty well. But she didn't say anything about his sister being Nygaard's wife."

"Right. Bring her in too. Right after him. Maybe we're getting somewhere." It was coming up to 5:30. Time to go home.

Harlow was exhausted. It had been a long day and travelling made it all the more tiring. He hated airports. He hated the long lineups. He hated all the security checks. At the top of his hate list, however, was all the wasted time. When he was a kid he had watched "The Jetsons" and thought their personal flying car would be a reality when he reached the ripe old age of fifty-five. The only thing flying now was time, and he was stuck in the warp bubble of life.

Lying on top of a comfortable bed in a cozy Victorian-style room, he ran through the events of the day, and realized that the moment he had stepped off the Twin Otter, he had stepped back in time to when he was a boy in Boothbay Harbor, Maine. The same salty air, same rugged coastline and same natural habitat. And the same feeling of small town America. He found he had slowed down to blend with the ambience. At this point, he didn't know if it was making him all the more languid or energized. No doubt a night of blissful sleep would bring him the answer.

Meeting the editor of *The Bayside Bugle* and chatting with the police chief and his two officers had been a revelation. They were straight-forward men, the kind found in his hometown. And his dinner with Teresa and Miguel Flores had brought to mind the best part of Latino California—his good friends from Boyle Heights in East L.A.

Then there were the Abernathys. He almost laughed out loud. They were caricatures of "ye olde England," if ever a place existed. Except for their politeness, they didn't seem to be a bit Canadian. He wondered why they ever left Britain. Perhaps it was because here in tiny Britannia Bay with other ex-pats they felt more at home than they would have in modern day Britain. The young man at "Fleet Street" wasn't wrong when he said they were a story in their own right. Harlow intended to include them in the book he was planning to write when he retired.

Right now, however, he had to write something for his bosses in L.A. He got up, opened his laptop and got busy with his work.

Downstairs in the kitchen, Clive and Daphne Abernathy were doing the thing they loved most—gossiping over tea and toasted crumpets. Every so often he would turn and give a bit of crumpet to Calvin, their brightly coloured conure. "Want a treat?"

The bird would echo, "want a treat," or a reasonable facsimile thereof, and continue walking back and forth on Abernathy's shoulder.

"Mr. Harlow is quite a natty dresser, don't you think, Clive?"

Abernathy agreed. "Perfect casual wear for a trip." He added a dollop of jam, and took another bite, speaking while chewing. Calvin uttered "want a treat," and tried to steal a speck from Abernathy's fingers. "All right, Calvin. That's quite enough." He put the bird on his perch and ordered him to stay there. The bird complied.

"What do you think he'll write?"

"It may be just a reiteration of what we read in the *Bugle*. As far as I can see, there's nothing *to* write. Not yet, in any case." He swallowed the last of the crumpet. "I say, Bryony has really perfected these, don't you think?"

"Hmm. Yes," she replied absentmindedly. "Do you think we should tell him that Nygaard stayed with us?"

Clive put down the cup of tea he was about to drink and glared at his wife. "Daphne. What have I said on this subject?"

She pressed her lips together and contemplated her wedding ring.

"We mustn't get involved. Game, set and match. Which reminds me. I must get in touch with Basil. The weather's become too beastly to play. The wind just sends the ball out of the court."

Daphne had her own opinion of why the ball went astray, but said nothing.

Harlow filed his brief report and hoped the next day would get him meatier results. He had a hot shower, put on his pyjamas and sank into a deep sleep. The last thing he heard was the wind whistling past his window.

Twenty-eight

Thursday, November 6th

Benson arrived on time and in a foul mood. "I want to know why I'm here again for more questioning. Isn't this some kind of harassment? I've got a good mind to contact a lawyer."

"You're welcome to do that, Mr. Benson. But you are not here under caution. This is merely a clarification of some facts that were omitted during your first interview," Wyatt explained.

"Perhaps it is, but I can't be dragged away from the set every time you want to *clarify* something."

"You could have remained on the set today if you had been more forthright during the last interview," Wyatt told him. "As it is, you left out something glaringly important."

"What was that?" Benson's eyes briefly shifted away.

"That Nygaard was your brother-in-law. That your sister, Bibi Benson, was married to him. And that he was arrested for assaulting her. Don't you think we should have known these details?"

"I didn't think they were relevant."

"How do you figure that?"

"Because I did not kill him. I didn't want to mention Bibi because you would have automatically assumed that I had killed him to avenge what he did to her. And that would've led to nothing but hassles for me."

"Doesn't it have a ring of truth to it?"

"It might. But it doesn't *point* to the truth. I am telling you now, once and for all, that I did not kill Berens Nygaard ... as much as I might have wished him dead. My sister always told me to stay out of their business. That the altercations were hers to deal with and she would take care of him in her own fashion. So I did as she asked."

"What do you think she meant by 'in her own fashion'?"

"I don't know. She may not have said those exact words. I was just told to butt out. She could look after herself."

"But you were keeping an eye on him to make sure he didn't pull any shenanigans while he was here. Isn't that right?"

"Yes."

Ray and Jimmy watched in the viewing room. "He seems credible, don't you think?" Ray asked.

Jimmy nodded. "He's either that or a great actor. I didn't see any tells."

Wyatt had completed his discussion with Benson, who left with his hackles still up.

"So, what did you think, fellas?" Wyatt asked them.

"We think he's innocent," Ray said.

"Me too. When is Brotman due?"

"Shortly."

"Okay. Jimmy and I will observe. You take the interview."

It was difficult for Ray to imagine Peggy Brotman cranky. He had watched the video of her with Jimmy and she was downright pleasant. Not today.

"I really hope this is the final time you need to talk to me."

"We really hope so too, Miss Brotman. During your interview with D.S. Tan, you said you knew Allen Benson pretty well." Ray knew she hadn't said that precisely, but he wanted to see if she would correct him. She did not.

"Yes. I suppose I do."

"Have you socialized with him out of working hours?"

Something flashed in her eyes. "I hope you're not suggesting that I'm having an affair with him!"

Ray realized his error. "No, I apologize. That's not what I meant. I was wondering if you've seen him in a social setting."

"Oh." Her umbrage ebbed. "Well, we've been at the Oscars, Golden Globes … you know, but not together. He was with the upper crust. But I'm puzzled by your question. Where is this going?"

"I was wondering if you had ever met Bibi Benson."

She nodded. "Yes. I met her once. It was just before we came up here."

"What was the occasion?"

"The Executive Producer was throwing a little do for the company at the Bel Air Hotel."

Ray wondered if she had twigged to the irony of the party being held at the same hotel as the assault. "So Miss Benson was at this do?"

"Yes." She paused. "She was gorgeous in person."

"Were she and Nygaard together?"

She took a minute. "They arrived together and posed for a few pictures. I didn't notice them together after that. But I was hanging out with my friends."

"Why didn't you mention that Nygaard and Benson were in-laws?" He said it with such force that it caused her to blink before answering.

"I assumed that Allen would have told you that."

That made sense to Ray. "Thank you very much, Miss Brotman. I don't see the need for you to come in again."

"That's it?"

"Yes, that's it."

"That's a relief. Are you any closer to finding out who did this?"

"Can't say anything about that," he said.

"No, I guess not." Her friendly disposition returned. "Okay then. Bye. And say goodbye to Sergeant Tan for me. He's cute."

In the viewing room, Wyatt smirked at Jimmy.

"Yeah. So what? I am."

Ray was waiting for them in the hallway. "Hey, cutie, let's have a chat."

As they hunched over a kitchen table and munched their lunches, they agreed that both Benson and Brotman seemed to be in the clear.

"Where do we go from here?" Ray asked.

"Since we've been talking about Bibi Benson, why not look at her Facebook page … see if anything pops up," Wyatt suggested.

Ray and Jimmy smiled. "Welcome to the twenty-first century, Pops."

Twenty-nine

Harlow had parked his car up the street from the house where the shoot was in progress. The wind had picked up overnight and was gusting across the chilly waters of Britannia Bay. He zipped up his jacket, slung his backpack onto his left shoulder and sauntered down past several large trucks to the driveway entrance and up to the posted guard. "Good afternoon. I'm Henry Harlow from the *Los Angeles Herald*." He handed his business card to the guard. "I'd like to speak to either Peggy Brotman or Allen Benson."

The guard scrutinized the card. "Do you have some picture I.D.?"

"Yes, just a second." He extracted his wallet from his backpack, removed his driver's licence and gave it to the guard.

"Okay." He handed it back but kept the business card. "Wait here." He walked away and made a call. The conversation was short. He made another call. Harlow saw him nodding as he answered some questions, giving him some hope.

The guard put his phone away and returned to Harlow. "Miss Brotman is coming out."

"Okay, thanks very much."

Harlow had perused the *Paradise Pines* website and seen a couple of pictures of Peggy Brotman, but he wasn't prepared for her small stature.

"Hi, Mr. Harlow. I wondered when the Hollywood press would arrive."

"Hello, Miss Brotman. Thank you very much for seeing me. And so far, I'm the only one."

"C'mon with me. There's a place we can sit away from this wind."

"It's pretty strong. Nothing getting blown away, I hope," he said amiably.

"No. We're doing interiors today." She walked past the house. Harlow tried to glimpse through the windows but they were blocked with black-out blinds. A tarp-covered swimming pool sat midway between the house and the edge of the property where a gazebo nestled among conifers and shrubs. Gigantic urns filled with ferns and colourful foliage sat on either side of the entrance. A rattan divan, two similar chairs and a low table filled the space. "We'll sit in here. It's kinda cozy."

There were a few minutes of uncomfortable silence as they sat opposite one another. "I'm surprised the paper sent you and not an arts reporter."

"I can understand that, but it *is* a news story."

"We've been reading the online papers and Twitter feeds and saw your report this morning. It was a lot less sensational than some of the others. But there wasn't much news in it." She smiled.

"There isn't much to report right now."

"At least you didn't put in any unsubstantiated claims from anonymous sources."

"That's not my style, Miss Brotman. I report the news. I don't make it up, as some do these days. And I'm not interested in the gossip side of the story. I think an arts reporter might be inclined to do those things."

"Perhaps." She rubbed her forehead and yawned. "I'm so tired. We're working flat out and everyone is exhausted."

"How's the morale?"

"Not that great. The new director is doing what he can to cheer us up. But when you have a murder in the company, it's hard to get past that."

"I imagine people are being wary and wondering if someone on the set is the killer."

She seemed taken aback at the suggestion. "We don't think it's one of us. We think his past caught up with him. His drug past. We think it's someone from Vancouver who had it in for him for some reason."

Harlow nodded. "Could be. Has Allen Benson mentioned anything about returning early to be with his sister?"

"Why should he? She's probably handling it pretty well. I don't see her as the weeping willow type."

"She may be relieved he's not around to beat her up anymore. Maybe Felix Feldman, too. After all, he does her makeup. No more black eyes to cover up."

Her eyes narrowed. "I thought you said you weren't into gossip."

"Touché," he smiled.

"Now, I have to get back to work. I'm already behind because the police had me in for more questions this morning. So if you will excuse me." She got up.

"Thanks for taking the time to see me."

She regarded him with a level gaze. "There's no story here, Mr. Harlow."

"Do you ever feel like a nobody?" Ray asked Jimmy.

They were sitting at Jimmy's work station scrolling through Bibi Benson's Facebook pages.

"Pretty well all the time. The only one who thinks I'm somebody is Ariel."

"Haven't you ever wanted to be famous … even for the legendary fifteen minutes?"

"Never. Fame is fleeting. See all these plastic people standing on the red carpet in front of Grauman's Chinese Theatre? How many of them will be remembered four hundred years from now, like Shakespeare or Bach?"

"You're assuming there's even going to be a world in four hundred years."

"Since we're playing let's pretend, then go with it."

"It's just that it would be fun to get all gussied up and have our pictures on the front page of a major publication."

"You, who don't even have a Facebook page," Jimmy said sardonically.

He brushed off Jimmy's barb. "Our names will never be up in lights. We'll never be on the Wikipedia website. The only mention of us will be in the obituary section of *The Bayside Bugle*."

"That's fine with me. Living under the radar has its merits. Who wants to be a source of gossip, especially when most of it's negative?" He paused, remembering the death of a young girl due to on-line bullying. "And sometimes murderous."

"Yeah, you're right." Ray rolled his shoulders and cracked his neck. "So, what're we looking for here?"

"I'll know it when I see it," Jimmy said. He stopped at the next page. "Like here." He pointed to a picture of a silver-haired gentleman standing close to Bibi Benson. They were both dressed in evening clothes and smiling, not at the camera, but at each other. He read the names in the caption. "Oh. This is Avi Rothman, the Executive Producer of *Paradise Pines* ... the person Harlow was referring to. The rich guy in the wings."

"Hmm. They look pretty tight, don't they?"

It was the next photograph that had them gaping at the screen. "Well, well. Isn't this interesting," Ray said.

"Let's see what's on *his* page," Jimmy said.

Felix Feldman's Facebook pages were so full of "best friends" that Jimmy had to scroll rapidly trying to find that one recognizable face. He stopped when he found it. Bibi Benson with Feldman—several shots of them hugging and mugging for the camera.

"I'll get Wyatt," Ray said.

"Take a look at these," Jimmy said, when Wyatt came in with Ray. They leaned over his shoulder and peered at the pictures and postings, pausing over the ones with Bibi Benson.

"Definitely *real* best friends," Ray began. "But for my money, he's a flaming—" he caught himself.

"Now, Ray," Wyatt warned. "We're going to have to talk to him again, so you'll have to bite your tongue. Jimmy, give him a call. See if you can get him in here today. What was your take when you interviewed him?"

"No alarm bells, chief. Just another crew member with an alibi."

"I wonder if he got the job on *Paradise Pines* because of his friendship with Miss Benson. Maybe Henry Harlow can give us a heads up before we talk to Feldman."

In the car, Harlow checked his messages and saw one from Chief Wyatt. Rather than call, he decided to drop in.

"Unfortunately, I didn't get any solid information from Peggy Brotman." Harlow sat with Wyatt, Ray and Jimmy in the kitchen, drinking coffee and chatting like old friends.

"Any incidental information?" Wyatt asked.

"Apparently they're willing to believe that the murder has something to do with his past drug use. No mention if he was still using. Some people are probably happy to have seen the back of him. But no one stands out."

"Not even Felix Feldman, the make-up artist?" Wyatt asked. "We've been doing some research into him and it seems he was particularly close to Bibi Benson."

"I brought up Felix Feldman with her, but she sidestepped my insinuation."

"You were looking at the Feldman angle, too? I thought you were a news reporter, not a gossip columnist," Ray said.

"That's what she called me," he laughed. "But you can't work in the media in L.A. and not be bombarded with all kinds of chit-chat about the motion picture and television industries. They take up a good portion of news reporting, for what it's worth. Bibi Benson, being a star, gets a lot of coverage. And because Feldman does her makeup—not just for her acting roles but also for her personal appearances—he gets a lot of exposure, too."

"So, what is he doing here in this small town working on a mediocre television show?" Ray asked.

"It's actually not that mediocre. But it's certainly not in a league with some of the long-running series that draw in most of the viewing audience. As for why he's working here rather than in a major production, your guess is as good as mine. If it turns out that he *is* the culprit, it'll be a sensational story," Harlow said, his normally calm demeanor showing some unmistakable sizzle. Brotman's final words had nettled him. He was hoping to toss them onto the trash heap.

Thirty

Feldman was in Victoria, a long drive south. He told them he couldn't *possibly* get back in time today for an interview. The earliest he could come in would be at ten in the morning. He had to do makeup first. But even with that disappointing news, Ray leered. "He's shopping for antiques," he simpered in a high-pitched voice and waved his hands about.

Jimmy shook his head in disgust. "*You're* an antique."

"I know. I'm an anachronism, according to Gabby. She thinks I'm a homophobic racist. Maybe I am, but I leave all that behind when I walk through that door. And most of it's an act, anyway. You know me."

Jimmy had to admit it was true. They had been partners for eight years now, and in all that time Ray had never allowed his personal prejudices to get in the way of his job.

Georgina was surprised at Ray's early arrival. "What brings you home at this hour?" Realizing she sounded put off, she decided to tone it down a bit. "Not that I'm not happy to see you. It's just unusual. That's all."

"Thanks for the underwhelming welcome, Georgie," he said, putting on his wounded look.

"Sorry, honey. Will you let me hug you as an apology?"

"Well, since you're dressed and ready to go to work, I guess it's the best I can expect." He opened his arms and then held her for a long while, rubbing her back as he did so.

"Oh, that feels good," she mumbled into his shirt.

"*You* feel good."

She began laughing and stepped back. "I could feel something else feeling good."

He grinned stupidly. "What do you expect? You're a hot babe." He moved to the kitchen counter and began his cappuccino ritual.

"So, why *are* you home so early?"

"We couldn't do much more today. But I think tomorrow will be a busy one. And if things pan out, we may be looking at a few days of activity." He took a slurp of his coffee. "Georgie, do you think I'm a homophobic racist?"

"Where is *this* coming from?"

"From Gabby. I think she's keeping a list of some of the things I say."

"No, Ray. I don't think you're a racist–as such. I mean, you some-times paint whole ethnic groups with a broad brush. But when it comes to individuals, you're not like that at all. As for being homophobic, you do have some of that going on."

Ray nodded. "I know. I can't help it. It's the ones who flaunt it publicly that put me off. Like those gay parades and all the queers dressed in drag and gyrating–you know, thrusting out their pelvises. It just makes me want to puke."

"But how do you feel about J.D.? I mean, she's gay."

"J.D. keeps her sexuality to herself. And she's so warm and kind. Even though you know she's gay, it doesn't make any difference. She gets under Carpenter's nose, though. But Tamsyn tore a strip off him about a comment he made."

"Now *there's* someone who *is* a homophobic racist!" she said vehemently.

"Who? Not Tamsyn!"

"No, you idiot. Carpenter."

"He's better than he was when he joined the squad. Even *I* thought he was way out of line sometimes."

"Are you worried about what Gabby thinks?"

"Yes, I am."

"Why don't you sit down and have a talk with her?"

"I would but I never see her anymore. She's usually getting ready for school when I leave for work, and then she's at Catalani's after school. When she comes home, she buries herself in her room doing homework."

"Then I will."

"Thanks, Georgie."

"You're welcome, you big galoot. I have to go now. Mamma made another *vincisgrassi* for your dinner. Don't eat the whole thing!"

"As if." They hugged one more time. Then she put on her coat and left.

He cut a large slab of the lasagna, nuked it and poured himself a glass of wine, all the while thanking the women in his life. Then he sat and ate. Alone.

Ariel was at the piano when Jimmy came home. He tiptoed by the music room and on to the den where he booted up the computer to Feldman's Facebook page. He began downloading the relevant pictures and comments onto his flash drive. After a while, the door opened. He swiveled around, not realizing the music had stopped.

"Hi, honey. When are you going to join the land of the living?"

He checked the time. "Holy cow! Is it this late already?"

"Dinner is about to be served. What are you doing that's keeping you so engrossed?"

"I'll tell you about it after I clean up and get some food into me."

"I know that we always talk about my day first," Ariel said. "But my news may spoil dinner."

"Nothing could be much worse than a murder, so go ahead. Why break with tradition?"

She grinned "Some tradition. Anyway, it seems my father's condition has worsened. Jeffrey called and he's urging me to go over. The last time he visited him, the old man confused him with his dead brother."

"What are you going to do?" Jimmy asked, knowing how she was wrestling with the problem.

"Nothing."

"Nothing?"

"Nothing. Unless Kate calls me and asks both of us to come over, I'm not doing anything." The use of her mother's name was not lost on Jimmy. It was a further indication of the damage created by space, time, and grievances.

"What if he dies, Ariel?"

"What if he does?" She didn't exactly jut out her jaw. But close.

When they were getting to know each other, Jimmy had run up against the stubborn streak that resided deep in her storehouse of idiosyncrasies. At times it served her well, for example, when she defied her parents to marry him. Or perhaps that served *him* well. At other times, it was a detriment. He wasn't sure if this would be one of those times.

"I know what you're feeling," he commiserated. "But if it comes to that, you'll wonder if he finally regretted what he said. And the wasted years. And you won't know that unless you talk to him face-to-face."

"If I don't hear from Kate, then I'll know he doesn't care. That's why I'm not going over."

Her dogged resolve ended his attempt at an intervention. It pained him. He knew she was hurting. The only help he could offer was to stay silent and support her.

They never did get around to his day, which got a whole lot better at bedtime.

Thirty-one

Friday, November 7th

It was one of those rare November days that people recall in later years. Temperatures soaring. Sun filling the sky. Dogs chasing frisbees on the beach. It was good to be alive.

Wyatt and Sherilee were at breakfast sharing a Western omelette and the latest news about their children. This part of his life brought him crazy pleasure, and when his grandson Benjamin crawled onto his lap, he struggled not to weep with love. He wished Luke and Ashley would have more children. He had given up on his daughter ever having any. Kellie said that being an elementary school teacher had given her enough kids to last a lifetime.

Sherilee sighed over the situation. "She's been dating this latest fellow for six months and so far she hasn't found anything to fault in him. So maybe there's still hope."

"Well, that's something, I suppose. But she's thirty. She has to be thinking about the ticking clock, don't you think?"

Sherilee nodded. "We'll just keep our fingers crossed. It's all we can do. And if she chooses not to have kids, then so be it. It's not the only legacy of one's life, after all."

"No. You're right about that. She's made an impact already." He got up. "That hit the spot, honey. Thanks. Now I've got to hit the road. Big day ahead."

"Good luck, Bill. I hope you make progress on this case today."

"Boy. So do I. These murders are taking a toll on everyone."

This time Felix Feldman eschewed his working garb of colourful T-shirt and tight jeans and arrived wearing a blue shirt under a black wool and leather bomber jacket much like those worn by any of the men at the station. His navy corduroy pants and highly polished loafers completed the image of any well-heeled conservative man. His razor-cut sun-streaked brown hair seemed to be naturally achieved and not the result of some salon wizardry, which meant it probably was. His blue eyes stood out against his tanned face.

He did not sashay to the interview room, causing Ray to wonder if perhaps he wanted to dispel the notion that he was an in-your-face homo. Contrary to what Wyatt had said, he would do the questioning, with Jimmy sitting in the corner and Ray and Novak in the observation room.

"I've already answered your questions," Feldman said testily, as he removed his jacket and took a seat.

"We just need more details concerning your movements on the night of the murder. You said you were at the beach. Do you have your own car?"

"No, I don't."

"How did you get there?"

"Eddie drove me. He has a rental car."

"That would be the Eddie Mankoff, the Props Master."

"Yes."

"When you were originally interviewed, you said you stayed to watch the fireworks program. That would have ended around ten o'clock or so."

"Well, actually I didn't stay for the whole thing because I had to drive Eddie back to the motel."

"Why was that?"

"He said he wasn't feeling well. He was dizzy."

Wyatt checked the file. "You didn't mention this."

"I forgot."

"That was quite a detail to forget, Mr. Feldman."

Feldman appeared abashed. "Sorry."

Wyatt stared long and hard at Feldman, who ran a hand over his head and looked away.

"What time *did* you leave the beach?"

"Um ... it must have been around nine thirty."

"And when you got back to the motel, what did you do?"

"I helped get Eddie to his bed. He just flopped on it. So I covered him with a blanket and went to my room."

"What did you do for the rest of the evening?"

"There *was* no rest of the evening. It was over, as far as I was concerned. So I turned in."

"What happened the following morning?"

"Eddie said he was fine, so we went to the set. And that's when we heard that Nygaard was dead."

"How did you hear about it?"

"We were all gathered around, wondering why he was late because he is always so punctual. Then Peggy told us that Angel had called with the ghastly news."

"Now, think carefully about what I am going to ask you. Was there anyone who didn't seem upset or surprised by the news?"

"What do you mean?"

"Well, there could've been one other person who knew before everybody else."

It took him but a nanosecond to comprehend Wyatt's implication. "You mean you think somebody from the company killed him?"

"If it is, who would be your first guess?"

Feldman shook his head. "I have no idea. And I don't remember anyone reacting strangely. I can't believe it would be one of *us*." He threw up his hands then rubbed his face. "This is all too much for me to process right now." Then he sat straight and looked directly at Wyatt. "I'm not under arrest, am I?"

"No, you're not," Wyatt said.

"Then I can leave."

"Yes, you can," Wyatt unhappily acknowledged.

"Do you have a ride back to the set?" Jimmy asked. "If not, we can drop you off."

Feldman noticed the officer sitting in the corner, and smiled at the small kindness. "No, thanks. I have Eddie's car."

They ended the interview and allowed him to go, with a caveat. "Keep your eyes and ears open, Mr. Feldman," Wyatt said. "If you learn anything that can help us in this investigation, contact us. And remember that there might be a killer amongst you."

Feldman shuddered, put on his jacket and walked out.

Ray joined Wyatt and Jimmy. "We need to talk to Mankoff again," he said. "He didn't say anything about being sick. It could have been a ruse. He could've used it as an alibi. If they were back at the motel at nine-thirty, that would have given him time to get to Nygaard's house, shoot him, and get back to the motel before others began to return from the beach."

"Just," Jimmy said.

"I think it's time we hauled Mankoff's ass in here," Wyatt said.

"Feldman has his car," Jimmy pointed out.

"Then maybe we should bring him in ourselves."

Jimmy shrugged. "Works for me."

"Let's give him a bit of a scare," Ray said, eyes gleaming. They changed into their uniforms, adding duty belts and firearms. After discussing how they were going to proceed, they headed out, *sans* sirens and lights.

Thirty-two

"If Mankoff is our man, he must have had a reason to top Nygaard," Jimmy said. "What was it, and why now? They'd been here less than two weeks. What happened?"

"And where do you think he got the weapon?" Ray wondered.

"And does he still have it?"

"If he kept it, he's toast," Ray said.

"Remember Jackson saying that Nygaard was watching everyone like a fox outside a henhouse?"

"Maybe it's about drugs after all. Maybe Nygaard twigged to what was going on and maybe he suspected Mankoff."

"Maybe that's who Nygaard was waiting for that night."

"Maybe he decides to have a meeting with Mankoff. Warn him off. But Mankoff realizes the money is too good, so he decides Nygaard is expendable." Ray pulled up behind one of the production trucks. "Here we are."

Crew members standing by the catering truck gawked at the sight of two cops in uniform, fully armed. As Ray and Jimmy walked briskly toward the entrance of the house, the security guard rushed up to them. "You can't go in there. They're filming."

Ray held up his badge. "Take a look at this. It's no prop." And muscled past him.

As they entered the room where filming was in progress, everyone stopped. With all eyes fixed on the doorway, the new director turned and saw the police.

"Cut! What in hell are you doing here?"

Ray held up his badge one more time. "Police business."

Surveying the room, they spied Mankoff sidling through to the dining room, and out the kitchen to the back door. They took off after him. Seeing glimpses of a tall fence behind a thick protection of tall trees and underbrush, they determined he wouldn't get far. But there were plenty of places to hide.

"Time to get a search party," Ray said, and radioed the station with the request. While they waited for reinforcements, they took opposite sides of the grounds and began poking through what was a mini forest. It was dusty work as dry leaves and pine needles dropped down, covering their caps and clothing. Not much later, they heard sirens. They ran back to the front of the property and saw Foxcroft, Dhillon, McDaniel and Novak running their way.

"Mankoff's in back somewhere," Ray said. "Spread out. And someone take the gazebo."

They sped off. On the large veranda, cast and crew had come out to watch. Mouths open. Eyes wide. This was no movie.

It wasn't long before the officers heard McDaniel shout, "Got him!"

Everyone ran to the gazebo.

McDaniel yanked Mankoff from his crouching position behind one of the huge urns. He and Novak pushed him face forward against a wall. Novak slapped on handcuffs.

"What are you doing?" Mankoff yelled.

"Placing you under arrest," Novak said.

"For what?" he shrieked.

"Right now, it's for trying to elude the police," Ray told him. "That was very suspicious, don't you think? Oh, and by the way, you're also under suspicion for the murder of Berens Nygaard."

"Are you nuts?" Mankoff screamed. "I had nothing to do with that!"

"Then why were you doing a runner?"

Mankoff clammed up.

"Right. We'll have a little talk at the station, then, shall we?" Ray said.

As he was led away, Tiffany Blair approached Foxcroft. "I may have some information about Mankoff that you might find useful," she said quietly.

"Well, come on, girl. Let's take a ride in my buggy."

By the time they arrived at the station, Foxcroft had been given a rundown of Mankoff's activities, other than those for which he had been hired. She immediately relayed them to Wyatt, who got a search warrant for Mankoff's motel room and an impound order for his car. Then he and Jimmy began their interrogation of the suspect while Ray once again had the job of interviewing Tiffany Blair.

She started out by joking. "We have to stop meeting like this."

Ray laughed. "That's on the tape, you know."

"Well, a little levity lightens up all the dark stuff you guys have to deal with."

"True enough. So, Constable Foxcroft has told us that you believe drugs might be a possible motive for the murder of Berens Nygaard. Could you please detail your suspicions."

"Certainly. One day Flix, came into my dressing room–"

"–Flix?"

"Flix. The make-up guy. Felix Feldman, but everyone calls him Flix."

"Why?"

"Well, it's easier than saying Felix. And he flicks his hands around." She waved her arms around and laughed. "He's a character. Anyway, he strutted in and said something like, 'Here's the new wig you wanted,' in a sarcastic way, then flounced out as though he was annoyed with me. Well, I hadn't asked for a replacement. I didn't know what he was talking about. So I opened the box and took out the wig. It was identical to the one I had. Then I inspected the cap underneath and noticed how misshapen it was. It looked like someone had removed something from each of the small sections inside of it. The first thing I thought was cocaine in small cello packs."

"That's a pretty unusual thought, Miss Blair. Why would you think that? I heard that Nygaard wasn't using anymore."

"Oh, not Nygaard. He's clean, as far as I can tell. No. The other crew members. A lot of them use coke."

"And you think Mankoff was the supplier?"

"That's my guess. Angel has to drive me every day, and we talk. He just happened to mention that he and Eddie's assistant had made a fast run to the ferry for the wig. And when they got back, the assistant took it to Mankoff's trailer. Angel thought he would've taken it directly to Feldman. Then he figured Feldman could've been in Mankoff's trailer at the time. After then he didn't give it another thought. But I did."

"Why do you think Mankoff would kill Nygaard?"

"I think Nygaard caught on that someone was supplying coke to the crew and he was going to find out who it was and fire them. He didn't want any scandal touching *Paradise Pines*. Especially a drug scandal. Mankoff had a pretty good side deal going on and he probably wanted to make sure it stayed that way. He saw Nygaard as a threat."

Ray thought how similar her conclusions were to his and Jimmy's theory.

"So a new director would be a solution."

"That's my guess."

"Well, Miss Blair, I must say, you're missing your calling."

"Oh, what's that?"

"You would make a great detective."

She laughed. "As a matter of fact, I'm writing crime fiction on the side."

"I wondered about your facility for language."

"I'm not just another pretty face, you know. And it won't be like that forever. So I have to find another way to make my way in this dog-eat-dog world."

Ray followed the actress out of the interview room and noticed that Jimmy and the Chief were sitting in Wyatt's office. He led her to the front, said goodbye with thanks then joined his boss and partner. "What's going on?"

"Nothing much. Mankoff swears he was sick and that Feldman drove him back to the motel where he slept until the morning. He was adamant that he didn't kill Nygaard. But when we told him his motel room was being turned upside down searching for drugs and a gun, he shut up again. The duty counsel is on his way in. But it's Friday, so the earliest he can get a bail hearing will be Monday."

"Well, come and hear what Tiffany Blair just told me."

Afterwards, they agreed that it was enlightening. And entertaining.

"But what's Mankoff's connection to Vancouver? And *who* is his connection?" Wyatt asked.

Jimmy abruptly got up. "I'm going to make a phone call."

"Don'tcha just love it when he gets a bee in his bonnet?" Ray laughed.

They didn't have long to wait. He returned with a grin spreading across his face. "Peggy Brotman said that Mankoff worked with Nygaard in Vancouver ten years ago."

"Mm-hmm. So, maybe he was dealing back then, too," Wyatt said. "It would have been easy enough to find someone to supply him with whatever he wanted. And maybe Mankoff got in touch with that person again before coming here."

"Yeah. But ten years? That's a long time for a dealer to stay in business. Especially with all the gangs involved," Ray said. "If they don't get whacked by a competitor, they try to finesse the justice system. They all think they're fucking geniuses. Unfortunately, most of them have Jell-o for brains."

"It happens, though," Wyatt said. "You get someone high up in the chain with a good lawyer, and you can hang in there for quite a while. Think about Freeway Ricky Ross in L.A. In his prime he had over a thousand bagmen working for him. They all liked him. He treated them right. Maybe there's a guy in Vancouver like that. And maybe Mankoff somehow tapped into him."

"Well, maybe the Duty Counsel will talk some sense into him," Ray said. "Maybe waiting until Monday will give him some time to figure out what the rest of his life is going to look like."

Thirty-three

Austin Canfield, Duty Counsel, arrived. After a short, quiet one-on-one with Wyatt, he followed him to the holding cell. Mankoff looked up, flicked his eyes at the bald man with a briefcase, and glared at Wyatt. But otherwise showed no emotions. Wyatt left for the incident room.

Several off-duty officers had come by to take in the excitement. That the SOCOs found a quantity of cocaine, amphetamines, Valium and rohypnol in Mankoff's room had them hopeful. It would have been icing on the cake if they had found the gun. But no joy there.

"Well, at least we have something," Wyatt said. "Let's see if the DC has anything to say after his chat with Mankoff."

"He was smart to have rohypnol in his stash," Ray said. "You know what happens when you snort enough snow? You get anxious. Paranoid. But you can mitigate it with rohypnol."

Jimmy chuckled. "You're really making good use of that dictionary."

"Come off it, Tan. I did graduate from university, you know. It's just that I'm uncomfortable using words that make me sound educated."

"And it shows," Novak laughed.

Canfield knocked at the open door. "Captain Wyatt. He wants to talk."

His words were electric.

Wyatt rapped his fist on the table. "Right!" He jumped up. "I'll do the questioning. Ray, Jimmy, you observe. Novak, record. Everyone hang tight."

The order was a non-starter. Nothing short of an Act of God would have budged their behinds.

Mankoff now sat meekly, seemingly resigned to his fate.

"Your Duty Counsel has advised us that you wish to make a statement. Is this correct?"

"Yes."

"I'll be questioning you after. Do you understand?"

"Yes."

Wyatt then told Mankoff to proceed.

"I did not kill Berens Nygaard. The only thing I did was supply drugs to certain crew members—the ones that worked the longest hours. On Hallowe'en night, I was at the beach. I was passing out some stuff. Most of the crew was high by the time the pizza arrived. I had a couple of pieces and a beer. Then I got a godawful headache. Got dizzy. I told Flix—uh, that's Felix Feldman—to drive me back to the motel. When we got there, I could barely walk. The last thing I remembered was him dragging me into the room and dropping me on the bed. I didn't wake up till the morning. I had a sort of hangover. I took a couple of Tylenol. After a while I felt okay. Flix came and got me and we went to the set. Then we heard about Nygaard's death." He stopped and looked at Canfield, who gave a slight nod.

Wyatt waited then asked if he had any thing to add to his statement. Mankoff expelled a long breath. "Yes. I think someone slipped a roofie in my beer."

"Roofie, meaning rohypnol?"

"Right. It was one of the drugs I was selling that night."

"Why would they do that?"

"Maybe they thought it would be funny." He shrugged. "I don't know."

"Do you remember who you sold it to?"

"Sure, but that wouldn't have made any difference because people were trading stuff."

It was all Wyatt could do to stop shaking his head at the stupidity of that. "Did you tell anyone about your suspicions?"

"God no!"

"Why not?"

"Because I was waiting for someone to say something first."

"And in the meantime you were still going to sell it?"

"I hadn't decided. But it's one way to come down from a cocaine high."

"Do you have any idea who might have killed Mr. Nygaard?"

"No. I probably would've been a good suspect 'cuz I think he figured out I was dealing and was going to read me the riot act later that night."

In the other room, Jimmy turned to Ray. "Remember me saying it seemed like he was waiting for someone because there was pizza and a clean plate on the kitchen table?"

"Yeah. So you think he was expecting Mankoff?"

"Sounds like it."

"But then someone slips him a roofie–if what he says is true–and he doesn't make his appointment. So someone goes in his place. Someone who knew about his appointment."

"Maybe his good friend, Feldman," Jimmy said.

"Who better to slip him a roofie?"

"But what would be his motive?"

"That's the sixty-four-thousand dollar question."

During their brief back-and-forth, they had missed some of Wyatt's interrogation.

"Who's your supplier?" they heard.

An ironic smile curled Mankoff's lips. "I may take risks, but I'm not crazy."

Wyatt hadn't expected him to cough up the answer. But nothing ventured, nothing gained.

"Mr. Mankoff, do you own a gun?"

"No, I do not," he firmly answered.

With Mankoff having nothing more to say, Wyatt charged him with the possession and distribution of illicit drugs. As he began to explain what was next in Mankoff's arrest and arraignment, Canfield interrupted him.

"I've already laid out the steps, Captain Wyatt."

"Of course."

Wyatt ended the interview. Novak, who had been waiting outside, led Mankoff back to his cell. Canfield waited for Wyatt to gather up his papers, then spoke to him. "Mankoff knows that no one will be posting bail for him. He was pretty upset that he'll be spending his time in remand before entering a plea."

"I can imagine," Wyatt said, coolly. "Well, you break the law, you pay the price."

Canfield recognized a hard-nosed cop when he saw one. He nodded and left.

Wyatt, Ray and Jimmy discussed what they had heard.

"What surprised me was Mankoff's adamant denial of owning a gun," Jimmy said.

"Yeah. That rang true with me, too," Ray agreed.

"He may be lying about being sick. It would've been a good alibi because people would have seen that," Wyatt said.

"And don't forget, Nygaard owned a gun," Jimmy pointed out. "So Mankoff could have been counting on that."

"Well, you boys have got to either build a case against him, or look for another suspect."

During the night, Jimmy woke with a start. Something had tickled his brain when they had been looking at Feldman's Facebook page. It had come and gone. Now the itch was back. He extricated his arm from around Ariel and went to his computer. Several minutes later, cogs began shifting in his head.

Thirty-Four

Saturday, November 8th

Early the following day, the weekend team, plus Novak, assembled around the white board, now crammed with photographs and clippings. Wyatt inspected two shots showing a dissolute Peter O'Toole as King Henry II with four other actors dressed as knights in one, and Richard Burton dressed as Thomas Beckett, the Archbishop of Canterbury, in the other. Below was a quote from the movie: "Will no one rid me of this turbulent priest?"

"What's this, Tan?" Wyatt asked.

Jimmy weighed his words with care knowing that what he was going to say would sound weird, if not outright wacky. "I think these words from *Beckett* have an analogy to Nygaard's murder. The suggestion by King Henry was carried out by these knights who killed the Archbishop. He didn't outright say, 'go and murder this man,' but that's what he was implying."

"What's this got to do with Nygaard's murder?" Carpenter asked.

"Bear with me, Craig." He continued. "For me, it didn't add up that Felix Feldman would accept a job on a television series. According to Peggy Brotman—and from what I saw on his Facebook page—he only works on high-budget movies. That's been his bread and butter for several years."

Ignoring the frowning faces facing him, he pointed to the picture of Bibi Benson with Avi Rothman and explained who he was to the uninformed. Then he put up another picture. "Here are the two of them again, and this time Felix Feldman is with them."

"So what?" Carpenter asked, with his usual touch of impatience.

Jimmy knew he was in a minefield. But trusting his instinct, he pushed his premise forward. "I'm thinking that Bibi Benson took a page from *Beckett* and came up with a plan to get rid of Nygaard, using Feldman's loyalty and Rothman's love to facilitate it."

This bombshell left them stupefied and muttering amongst themselves.

Ray finally spoke. "Sorry, Jimmy, but it sounds too far out to me. Right out of a Hollywood movie … if you don't mind the *analogy*," he added with a smirk.

Jimmy ignored the jibe. "I know it seems way-out, but I did more searching. In fact, I was up most of the night. Here are some other things I found." He picked up print outs and posted them on the board. "Here's a shot of him back in his early career as an actor."

"An actor?" Wyatt questioned.

"Yes. And look who's in the background."

They peered at the old black and white reproduction. "That's Bibi Benson," Foxcroft said.

"That's right. And the article alongside dates it as nineteen ninety-seven. That's twenty years ago."

"So they've been associated that long," Wyatt said.

"More than associated." He tacked up a reprint from an old *Hollywood Reporter*. "Here's Feldman graduating from the Max Factor School of Aesthetics. And see who's standing beside him? She's been a supporter of his career all the way. Probably helped him get a foot in the door."

"This is nothing short of diabolical, Tan," Wyatt said.

"And why do it? What would he get out of it?" Carpenter asked. "I mean, this is murder, man."

"Other than her loyalty, maybe something big for him in the future. With Avi Rothman in Miss Benson's pocket, who knows what they could promise Feldman? Maybe an Oscar? I think we should call him back for questioning right away. He'll probably think he's in the clear after hearing that Mankoff's been arrested."

After an interlude of silence as they mulled over the scenario, J.D. Dussault cleared her throat and raised her hand. "I have a tiny off-the-wall observation."

"Go ahead, J.D.," Jimmy said.

"You may have the right quote, but in this case it should have been uttered by Lady Macbeth."

Jimmy smiled. "Right on."

A few officers looked at her with interest.

Wyatt, who had remained silent, finally nodded. "Okay. There's enough of a suspicion here to bring him back in. If we can't get a confession when we tell him what we've got, we may at least rattle him."

Feldman *was* rattled. He was left alone for a few minutes while Novak and Ray watched from their vantage point. Feldman's head turned left, then right, then around the room. When his hands weren't wringing, they were massaging his bobbing knees or correcting the crease on his pants when he crossed and recrossed his legs. "Looks like a drunk is controlling the puppet strings," Ray said.

As soon as Wyatt and Jimmy walked in, Feldman's pent-up emotion exploded. "Why am I here *again*? This is the *third time*!"

"We are just filling in background information," Wyatt said.

"What sort of background information? And am I being recorded as well?" He became wary.

"You may remember that we videotaped your last interview. We record all the interviews to protect everyone. I'm sure you understand that. Do you have any objections to it?"

It took a while for Feldman to answer. "No. I suppose not," he said through a pout.

"All right then. It is Saturday, November eighth …" and he continued with the preamble.

Feldman's demeanour changed knowing he was in the camera's sights. He got control of his mannerisms, sat up straight and looked directly at Wyatt.

"How did you get hired for this production?"

"Oh … uh, I was man hunted."

In the observation room, Ray whispered, "I'll bet," earning an elbow from Novak.

"What do you mean by that?" Wyatt asked.

"I mean *they* came to *me*. I didn't apply for the job," he huffed. "I am well known and have a reputation for doing some of the best work in the industry."

There was that word again, thought Wyatt. It irked him that making movies was called an industry. But then again, it probably did drive a lot of the economy in California.

"If you are so well known, I imagine you get some plum jobs."

Jimmy caught Feldman preening.

"Well, yes, I do. "

"Do you often go out of the country to work on a film?"

"No. This is only the second time. I did a shoot in England a few years ago."

"No problems getting a work visa this time around?"

"No. I was surprised that we needed one, that's all."

"Why is that?"

"Oh, you know. Canada and the US … we're so intertwined that we almost forget Canada's a foreign country," he tittered.

It was at this point that Ray noticed Feldman flick his hand out. He almost said something to Novak about the gesture and giggle but decided to keep his mouth shut.

"Why would you take a job on a television series that probably doesn't pay as much or have the same, shall we say, cachet?" Jimmy asked.

"As it happens, I thought I had a job lined up on a major motion picture, then all of a sudden they decided to go with someone else. I was really upset. But then I got this offer, so I took it. It seemed like fate."

"And I'm guessing knowing the right people helped," Jimmy said.

"I suppose so."

"Who actually hired you?" Wyatt took up the questioning again.

"The producer."

"When were you hired? The show has been going on for a year, yet it sounds like you're new."

"Yes. I was brought on this season."

"Do you know why?"

"The last person didn't want to be separated from his family. At least that's what I heard."

"Now I want to ask you about your friendship with Bibi Benson."

"What?" His voice rose.

"We're interested in your friendship with Bibi Benson."

"What has my friendship with Miss Benson got to do with anything?"

"Well, first of all, she's Allen Benson's sister."

"So?" he asked belligerently.

"As it turns out, she's not only a very close friend of yours but she's also a close friend of Avi Rothman, the Executive Producer of the show."

Moisture began to dot Feldman's forehead.

Wyatt continued, apace. "Don't you think it's interesting that you were hired for this production knowing that you were a friend of Miss Benson … someone who possibly hated Berens Nygaard?"

He licked his lips. "I don't know what you're getting at."

"You have spent a good deal of your professional life with Bibi Benson. From your Facebook page, it would appear in your personal life as well," Jimmy challenged him.

"You've been looking at my Facebook page?" His voice squeaked, jumping an octave.

"We have looked at everyone's social media sites," Wyatt lied. "And that includes Bibi Benson's."

"You seem to be long-time friends," Jimmy added. "So I imagine she's shared a lot of her personal problems with you over the years. Did she ever make any disparaging comments about her husband?"

"Well, she would complain about him. You know, his drug use, and chasing starlets."

"That's all?" Wyatt asked.

"She was really pissed off when she wound up with a black eye after one of their arguments. I was doing her makeup for a shoot and we had to delay her scenes because all the concealers in the world wouldn't camouflage the bruise."

"She never suggested that she would like to see the back of him?" Jimmy asked.

By this time, the quick questions and comments coming from one officer and then another, were wearing on Feldman. "One time she said she wished he would do a fade."

"I imagine her life will be a lot nicer without him around," Jimmy said.

Feldman tried laughing. "I imagine it will be."

"And she'll have you to thank for that, won't she?" Wyatt said.

Feldman recoiled. "What are you suggesting?"

"I'm *suggesting*," Wyatt began, "that Miss Benson dropped a great big hint that she would like her husband done away with. I'm *suggesting* that she and Avi Rothman were having an affair and that they saw a way clear to get rid of Nygaard by having you work on *Paradise Pines*."

"And somewhere between Hollywood and here, Bibi Benson convinced you to kill her husband," Jimmy said, bluntly.

"Are you totally mad? Like everybody else, I found out the following morning that he was dead."

"Tell us again what you did after you drove Mankoff back from the beach."

Feldman repeated his actions. Then sat silent waiting for another question. When none was forthcoming, he asked one of his own. "Is that all?"

Jimmy glanced at Wyatt, who shook his head. "Yes, that's all." He terminated the recordings and Feldman walked out. Only this time he sashayed.

Ray joined Wyatt and Jimmy.

"Damn!" Wyatt exploded. "How did I fuck up?"

"You didn't take acting lessons, Chief," Ray said.

"But going in, you weren't sure he would cave, Chief," Jimmy tried mollifying him. "And you did shake him up."

"Thanks for that bit of cheer, Tan. But you're right about his state of mind right now. I think we'd better alert the airline in case he tries to bolt."

Thirty-five

Jimmy felt his failure to nail Feldman as keenly as Wyatt had. He spent the rest of the afternoon reading over the most salient points concerning times and actions. There didn't seem to be anything there by which to arrest the man. Over dinner, he shared his thoughts with Ariel, who was distressed over his distress.

"Why don't you go back to the very beginning, Jimmy? To the first person you spoke to."

"You mean Quentin Pickell?"

"Well, if that's who it was. It's been a while. Maybe something has come back to him in the meantime. Or maybe just talking to him again might jog his memory."

He knew that minutiae often kicked in long after an event. "You're right." He considered the time. "I wonder if he would mind me calling on a Saturday night."

"I think Pickell would be tickled to know he's that important." She grinned, purposely mispronouncing his name.

Jimmy groaned. "It's a good thing he can't hear you."

But she was right about one thing. "I'm available right now, if you want to drop by," Pickell said, excitement in his voice. "Or do you want me to come to the station tomorrow?"

"If you don't mind the imposition, could I come to your house right now?"

"No imposition at all, Sergeant Tan."

He walked the few blocks, feeling refreshed by the crisp evening air. He hoped the case would be refreshed as well.

Pickell was waiting. Standing at his side was his wife, whom he introduced as Elizabeth. Her enormous brown eyes, round cheeks and cupid's bow lips reminded him of someone, but the image was elusive.

"I'm so glad to meet you, Sergeant Tan," she greeted him in a child-like voice.

The effect was almost comical, and he caught himself from smiling broadly. "Thank you for seeing me."

"We're only too glad to help," Pickell said, ushering him into the living room.

"Yes. Please sit down, Sergeant," his wife said.

The room was comfortable, homey. Flickering flames danced in the gas fireplace. The lighting was soft, subdued. Jimmy relaxed into an overstuffed chair, and had he not come on a mission, he might have dozed off.

"I know it's a little unorthodox, but I need to go over the night of Nygaard's death again."

"That's fine," Pickell nodded.

Jimmy took out his notes. "According to what you said that evening, you heard the shots at approximately nine forty-five."

"That's right."

"You presumed they were firecrackers and so you looked out the window, saw the lights out at Nygaard's and returned to watching the film."

"That's correct."

"I'm wondering … has anything come to you since then? Did you happen to hear any other noises?"

Pickell thought for a moment or two. "No," he said, shaking his head.

It was then that Elizabeth Pickell spoke a single word. "Oh." Her inflection was pregnant with meaning.

A frisson of excitement ran down Jimmy's spine. "Did you hear something, Mrs. Pickell?"

"Yes, now that you mention it. I wasn't in the den with Quentin. I was in the kitchen putting food down for Mitzy. That's our cat. First of all, I heard a car drive up. I thought it was Mr. Nygaard returning from some place … perhaps the beach. I was putting the can of cat food back in the fridge when I heard the shots. Of course, like Quentin, I thought they were firecrackers. I looked out the window and noticed that Nygaard's house was dark. I assumed he had turned out the lights and gone to bed. Then I saw a car drive away. I thought he'd received a ride from someone because I've never seen a car parked there."

"Mrs. Pickell, how could you hear a car drive up when your husband was in the next room watching a film?"

"Because I had to open the door for Mitzy to come in. That's when the car arrived."

Pickell turned to his wife. "Elizabeth, why didn't you tell me all this?"

"Because my mind was on other things, Quentin. If you remember, I was going over to the mainland to see my sister, and I was making a list of things to do in my head. It simply didn't register."

"This could be very important information. Would you be willing to come to the station early tomorrow morning and make a formal statement?"

Her wide eyes grew even wider. Her hand went to her throat. "Oh, my. Really? Well, yes. Of course I would."

Jimmy was jubilant. After thanking them profusely, he set up an appointment time, rushed home and got on the phone to Wyatt and Rossini. Then he turned to Ariel. "How do you do it? How do you always come up with a brainwave?"

"Well, we angels have our ways," she said, grinning, and giving him a sidelong look.

Thirty-six

Sunday, November 9th

Overnight, the sky lowered itself to the ground. In the morning, thick, white mist rolled in from the bay. Seagulls swooped and dove, their plaintive calls swept away by the wind. Air smelled of wood smoke. The short days of November were making themselves known.

The weekend shift was uniformly startled when Ray and Jimmy arrived on a Sunday morning at eight thirty, followed right after by Chief Wyatt, who made for the coffee maker.

Carpenter couldn't control his curiosity. "What's up?"

"It might be the proverbial break in the case," Ray said.

"How come?"

Before Ray could answer, the doors opened and in stepped Quentin and Elizabeth Pickell. He, confident. She, diffident. Robyn informed Wyatt, who took one slurp of his brew, regrettably left his cup on the kitchen counter and came to the front. "Good morning Mr. and Mrs. Pickell. Thank you for coming in. Would you like to follow me?"

As they passed by the crew, Drew Hastings did a double take at the sight of Elizabeth Pickell. After they entered the interview room, he said, "Well, if it isn't Betty Boop in the flesh."

"Who's Betty Boop?" Foxcroft asked.

"Oh, stop trying to prove how young you are, Tamsyn. Look her up on the Internet."

Adam Berry took the opportunity to imitate her voice. Everyone but Foxcroft laughed.

"That's pretty good, Adam," Hastings said.

"They make quite a couple," Carpenter said. "He looks like a kewpie doll and she's a cartoon character."

Foxcroft frowned. "But maybe they're the reason for the break in the case. So we shouldn't be making fun of them."

"You know what, Foxcroft? *You're* no fun!" Carpenter retorted.

Ray and Wyatt had already pegged who Elizabeth Pickell resembled. Jimmy was still in the dark, but fascinated by her all the same. They were locked up for about twenty minutes, recording her statement. When they exited, it appeared that the words of appreciation had already been spoken as the Pickells made straight for the front door. Wyatt returned to the kitchen and zapped his cold coffee.

"Well, there goes Betty Boop," Ray said.

"Oh, that's who it is!" Jimmy exclaimed.

"I'm proud to say I've never heard of her," Foxcroft said, dismissively.

Jimmy laughed. "Good one, Tamsyn." He got himself a cup of coffee then began going through a list of room assignments at the motel. "Ray, come here for a sec. What do you think about questioning Arellano further? His room is right next to Feldman's. Maybe he heard something because according to his statement he was back at the motel around ten fifteen. What do you think?"

It took a some convincing, but Ray finally agreed, although with a few reservations. "I wonder if they're shooting today."

Foxcroft piped up. "Yes, they are. I drove by the house on the way here."

Arellano was not happy being called away from the set. "What have you brought me in for anyway? People are beginning to look at me funny."

"Maybe we just like you, Angel," Ray replied, chuckling.

"Ha ha. Yeah, right." He smoothed over his flippancy with a smile.

"We just need to check a tiny thing, so would you mind reacquainting yourself with our interview room?"

"Oh. So not such a tiny thing if you're going to record me again."

"It may be tiny, but it's important," Jimmy said.

They got comfortable and after the recording started Ray queried him about his movements on Hallowe'en night. "You said you left the beach at about ten o'clock."

"That's right."

"Did you take anyone with you?"

"Yes, because not a lot of people have their own cars."

"Who were your passengers?"

He listed off three names.

"So, not Nygaard?"

"Nygaard?" he asked, bemused. "No. He wasn't at the beach."

"Right. Now, when you returned, what did you do?" Ray asked.

"I went to bed."

"I should clarify that. Before you went to bed. Step by step."

"Oh. Okay. After I parked my car, I thought I would see if Eddie was all right. I knocked on his door, but there was no answer. I figured he was asleep."

"Did you knock on Felix Feldman's door?"

"No. There was no light on. So I figured he was asleep, too."

"What did you do next?"

"I was on my way to my room … oh, right. Step by step. I remembered that I left my coffee thermos in the car. I went back to get it. It was dark and I stumbled against Eddie's car. I park next to him." He stopped. "Wait a minute! I just remembered something … something that seems kinda strange, now that I think of it."

"What was that?" Jimmy asked.

"When I put out my hand to straighten up, I noticed that his car was warm."

Ray and Jimmy exchanged a glance.

Arellano continued, doubt in his voice. "It shouldn't have been because he left the beach about an hour before." Then he perked up. "Or maybe Flix drove the car to a drug store to get something for Eddie. Maybe that's why." He was nodding his head by then.

Knowing that no drug store, in fact, *no* store was open after nine o'clock in Britannia Bay, Ray asked Angel what time that was.

"Um. Probably ten thirty."

"Anything else strike you as odd?"

"No."

"Okay. That will do it." Ray signed off.

Arellano was surprised. "That's all?"

"That's all."

"Just one thing," Jimmy interjected. "Is everyone on the set today?"

"Yes. It's our last day there."

"Thank you again for your co-operation."

"You're sure you don't need to see me again?"

"Only if we miss you," Ray said.

"You're a real comedian," he said, laughing as he left.

"He's a sweet kid," Ray said. "A suet pudding between his ears, but likeable."

"So, the car was still warm."

"Right. The exterior wouldn't have been warm after being shut off for an hour. And Feldman said he went to his room and turned in."

"That proves he was lying. He drops Mankoff off at nine thirty. Takes the car. It's about five minutes from the motel to Nygaard's. He shoots him at nine forty-five and is back at the motel by ten o'clock. So there was maybe less than a half hour or so before Arellano touched his car."

"I hope we've got him this time," Ray said.

"We're going to have to draft an information to charge him."

"Okay, let's get busy."

Well before noon, they had completed the document.

"Now we just need a summons or arrest warrant," Jimmy said.

"You know what that means, don't you? It means Judge Silverman." Ray's mouth made a moue. "You tell the Chief. I don't want him biting off my head."

When Jimmy presented the information and the sworn evidence document to Wyatt, the Chief looked at his watch. "Oh, joy," he sighed. "Sunday morning. The judge is going to be on the golf course."

At mid-morning, a veil of drizzle dropped down, enveloping the town. Delilah took one look out the window, picked up her Bible, and sat at the kitchen table, Tabitha curled in her lap. It was comforting having the little calico to keep her company. Especially when she couldn't go to church. She felt bad about missing the service, but she was sure Pastor John would understand. Being out in the wet with her walker was bad enough. But she didn't like to be dependent on drivers from the congregation. It meant having to be at their mercy after the service when she liked spending time in the downstairs community room chatting and eating sweets. There was a church service on a radio station from across the border starting up in a while. She would tune in to that. They always had nice hymns and no one would have to listen to her raspy old voice.

She flipped open the book, as was her habit, knowing that no matter where it landed, there would be an important message. It fell open to Ephesians Chapter Four. She noticed that verses thirty-one and thirty-two were underlined. She read them. "Hmm. That's interesting, Tabitha. I wonder why I was given this message today?"

Judge Mort Silverman felt his mobile vibrating as he and his caddy were trying to figure out what to do with the iffy lie. He was already teed off with the weather, and a call could only mean one thing, further firing up his ire. "Waddaya want, Wyatt?"

"A warrant for an arrest."

"What's the charge?"

"First degree murder."

Silence. "You got your man?"

As succinctly as he could, Wyatt explained the case so far.

"Hmm. Reasonable and probable grounds. Okay. Fax me over the documents and I'll get it to you ASAP. Didn't like the possibilities for my next shot anyway. Is your suspect still in the area?"

"He was as of a few minutes ago. The shoot winds up today, according to our source."

"Okay. Give me his name."

"Felix Feldman." Wyatt began spelling it out.

"Don't worry. Feldman I know how to spell." The line went dead.

Wyatt turned to Ray and Jimmy. "All right. Put on your gear and get your people together."

"Yes!" Ray pumped his fist.

This time, no film personnel stood around outside in the chilly rain to witness the arrival of several police vehicles. This time, the guard wisely stepped aside. Jimmy signalled for Berry, Hastings and Foxcroft to flank out, while he, Ray and Carpenter entered the house.

Inside, some members of the crew were standing behind a small group seated in a semi-circle, the director addressing them. He broke off in mid-sentence as the police filed in. Ray pinpointed Feldman in a chair. He walked directly to him. "Stand up, Mr. Feldman."

"Why?" he challenged them. When he remained seated, Ray nodded to Carpenter, who planted his linesman-like bulk beside the chair.

"I said, stand up," Ray repeated.

"Oh, all right!" Feldman snapped.

Carpenter instantly took hold of his arms. Feldman futilely tried to snatch them free.

"Let me go!"

Carpenter slipped on the cuffs, then gripped an elbow.

"What the hell?" Feldman yelled.

"You're under arrest." Ray began.

"For what?"

"For the murder of Berens Nygaard."

Gasps reverberated around the room.

"You're crazy!" Feldman shouted. "This is a mistake!"

"You have the right to retain counsel," Ray calmly advised him.

With that, Carpenter steered him out of the room as he continued to protest.

Ray turned to the astonished faces. "Th-th-th- that's all folks."

Thirty-seven

Monday, November 10th

The entire Rossini clan was gathered around the table for an early breakfast. Silvana and Umberto had arrived with a basket of warm cornetto. Georgina kept turning out egg and prosciutto open-face sandwiches and brought out Catalani's leftover biscotti for dipping into their cappuccinos. They were celebrating the visit of Marcus–his first time home since university started up in September. Georgina wanted to know about his studies. Gabby wanted to know about his girlfriends. And Umberto and Ray wanted to know about his success at soccer. No one wanted to know about the murder.

Silvana sat back, taking it all in with a full heart.

After an hour or so, Marcus asked about Lana. "How's she doing, anyway?"

Eyes rolled and glances were exchanged. "What?" he dragged out.

"Seems the new sous chef has been cooking up more than osso bucco," Ray smirked. "He's got her all steamed up."

"I think we're going to lose her," Georgina said.

"What do you mean by that?" Marcus asked.

"I think he's going to take her back to Italy next year. His visa will be up then, and she's going to have to make a decision pretty soon because there will be lots for her to do if she plans on leaving Britannia Bay," Silvana told him.

"Has she said anything?"

"She doesn't even think we know any of this. They think they are hiding their romance … the fools," Silvana said, but without rancour.

"What do you think of him?"

"He's a gentleman. Helpful. Even tempered …," Georgina began.

"Which is amazing considering he's a chef *and* an Italian," Umberto added.

"He has a good background, too," Silvana said.

"How do you know that? Did Leonora say so?"

At that, everyone became silent or suddenly busy with their biscotti. Marcus looked from one to another. "Okay. What's going on?"

Umberto spoke up. "Your grandmother had Josefina hire a private detective to look into him."

Marcus burst out laughing. "Oh, my God! What a family! Are you kidding me?"

Ray shook his head. "For real."

"What did he find out?"

"The guy has some credible bona fides," Ray said.

"What's that supposed to mean?"

"Let's just say that Lana could do a lot worse than hook up with this guy for good."

"So, he's loaded. Is that it?"

"He is from an established family with old money," Silvana told him.

"I don't want to her to go!" Gabby cried out. "She's been a good friend and helped me so much."

"Maybe we should pray to the Madonna for some kind of miracle to keep her here," Silvana said solemnly.

"Stop while you're ahead, Mamma," Ray said and rose from the table. "Speaking of that, I've got a big day ahead."

Feldman had been wakened, given a small breakfast, and whisked away by two marshals to await his appearance before Judge Silverman. A legal aid lawyer had been assigned his case. That afternoon, having read the evidence presented by Crown Counsel, and the possibility that he would be a flight risk, Silverman denied Feldman bail and he was remanded in custody.

"Well, that'll keep him tied up for a while," Wyatt said when Silverman's clerk phoned with the information.

"And we'll have to be prepared to appear if he pleads not guilty," Jimmy said, morosely.

"Let's see what the lab finds on his clothes. There might be traces of Nygaard's blood on some pieces," Wyatt said.

Ray almost growled. "I for one can't wait for this case to be over and done with. Give me the daily grind any day."

"Unfortunately that includes standing around tomorrow in the rain while the speeches are being read and wreaths laid," Wyatt said.

"If it rains," Ray said.

"Oh. It'll rain, all right. Happens every Remembrance Day," Novak said.

J.D. Dussault was down–her desultory mood compounded by the pounding rain. As she pondered her life, she wondered if she should get a dog. A dog would give her unconditional love–something she was missing in her life. But her job precluded that. A dog needed constant attention. A dog was expensive. A dog needed training. Maybe a cat. A cat didn't need a lot of attention, especially if it could entertain itself. And she wanted to redo the kitchen. She was handy and could do most of the work, and it would keep her occupied. But her take-home pay prevented the purchase of the big-ticket items she longed for–a counter-top gas range and a new dishwasher. Her musings were cut short by Chief Wyatt.

"Can you come into my office, J.D.?"

His brusque manner unnerved her. She sheepishly walked to his office avoiding the stares of her colleagues. Had she done something wrong? When he invited her to sit down and was polite about it, she relaxed a bit.

"J.D. I'm giving you a promotion."

She gawped at him. "A promotion? Really?"

"I don't bandy about words like that. I've–actually *we*–Mary Beth and I, have been looking at the budget and found a lot of places where we can cut incidentals and extras. So you'll get a raise commensurate with your new rank. You'll be a Constable Second Class and that will bump up your salary to …" and when he gave her the figure, she beamed. Now she could afford to redo her kitchen *and* consider a cat.

"This is wonderful, Chief. Thank you so much. But I'm sorry you had to cut out other stuff to make it happen."

"Don't worry about it. They weren't necessary for the operation of the station. As for your rank, you'll be on equal footing with Quinn, now. So don't let him go pushing you around," he said.

"He never did, sir," she said, taking him seriously.

Wyatt laughed. "He wouldn't dare. Now, march back to your desk with your head held high."

She got up and saluted. "Yes, *sir!*"

That made his day.

Thirty-eight

Tuesday, November 11th

Remembrance Day and, as prophesied by Novak, rain was sluicing down. By early morning, anyone who was anyone knew an arrest had been made. The unaware, however, were just waiting for *The Bayside Bugle* to be delivered. What was the holdup? They had no idea that Kittridge and his team had been up all night rushing to prepare a revised edition. He had gathered together the facts and added some snippets of gossip that had been simmering on the back burner. That should satisfy the madding crowd, he thought.

By mid-morning, the reason for the delay was broadcast about Britannia Bay, spread throughout the island and arrived across the water to the rest of the country. Kittridge called Harlow, who listened, banged out a story and fired it off to the *Los Angeles Herald*. Now, Hollywood and the western world would know.

Gordon Greenwood had had a brilliant idea, but now the weather had put the kibosh on it. He was going to take Eileen to Heritage Gardens for lunch. Now what could he do? An idea popped into his head. Searching his cupboards and refrigerator, he realized he could make lunch. For four.

Jimmy was placing the breakfast dishes in the dishwasher when the phone rang. Ariel got up from the table and answered. "Hi, Gordon!" She waited a minute or two. "That sounds delightful. We'd love to come. I'll bring dessert ... What time? ... Okay. We'll be there.

Looking forward to seeing you." She hung up. "Gordon has invited us to lunch. Eileen will be there, too."

"That'll be nice. It's been a while since we've sat down with them."

She hardly heard him. "I've got to figure out what I can whip up for dessert. Are you finished?" She elbowed him out of the way.

"I'm outta here," he laughed.

Lunch had become a laugh fest with Gordon relating tales of real estate transactions that were anything but cut and dried. "Some people can surprise you." He grinned. "One woman wanted to know if I would cut down an old poplar that was dropping leaves on one corner of the lot. I told her the birds used it as a home, and in the fall it had glorious yellow leaves and they made a beautiful whispering sound when the wind blew. So, no, I would not cut it down. And if the sale depended on that, then I would rather not sell the house to her. Then she flabbergasted me. She said that if I had agreed to chop down the tree, she wouldn't have bought the house. Apparently it was some kind of test. She was thrilled that there was someone else who treasured trees."

"As far as I'm concerned, you are few and far between. People are ripping out trees right and left around Britannia Bay. In our own neighbourhood, a woman had three gorgeous poplars cut down that had been there forever. She's new to the area so she probably doesn't understand why no one will speak to her anymore."

"I was surprised you stayed in the real estate game," Jimmy said. "I thought you would toss in your keys after the situation with the Schwindt house."

Ariel shot him a look. *That'll put a damper on things. Why did he have to bring that up?*

But Greenwood confounded her. He laughed. "It seems as though my properties are becoming havens for murders."

Eileen had been quiet during most of the hour. "But isn't it funny how quickly that house sold? Seemed like the people were fascinated by its infamy."

Greenwood nodded. "And there was Gunther Schwindt fretting about it, thinking it would never be sold. Strange how things turn out."

"Can I interest anyone in dessert?" Ariel asked, wanting to divert attention to something pleasant.

When they were on their way home, Ariel wasted no time in pouncing on her husband. "Why*ever* did you bring up the murders, Jimmy Tan? We were having such a nice conversation. Can't you for one minute forget that you're a cop?"

Jimmy drove a short distance before replying. "No. I guess I can't. It's just the nature of the beast."

Ariel puffed out a lot of air. "Oh, for God's sake!"

"Why are you so cranky, Ariel? It's not like you."

She could have given him some psychological mumbo-jumbo about her family situation, but just the thought of putting it into words exhausted her. Instead she apologized. When they arrived home, they were barely out of the car when they saw Delilah, covered in her plastic poncho, pushing her walker towards them.

"What's wrong, Delilah? Are you all right?" Jimmy asked.

She panted out a broken answer. "Had to see you right away. I'm okay." Then she turned to Ariel. "But it seems you're not, my dear."

"What?" an astonished Ariel replied.

"Let's get inside out of this rain. I have something to show you."

Jimmy hung up the wet coats, then cranked up the heat while Ariel and Delilah settled themselves at the kitchen table. Delilah took a book out of shopping bag. It was leather-bound and worn.

Ariel bristled at the sight of the Bible.

"Now, I know you're not religious, Ariel," Delilah said, looking at her friend and neighbour with soft, kindly eyes. "But something strange happened on Sunday, and I had to let you know what it was."

Jimmy put on water for tea and listened.

"I have this habit of letting the Bible fall open to wherever it wants and there's usually some message there for me. But I didn't understand why I got this one. Then later on I fell asleep and when I woke up, I remembered another message coming to me. It was that the words weren't for me. They were for you." She opened the big print Bible and read aloud. "Let all bitterness, and wrath, and anger, and clamour, and evil speaking, be put away from you, together with all malice. And be ye kind one to another, tenderhearted, forgiving one another, even as God for Christ's sake hath forgiven you."

Delilah's reading upset Ariel, who rose and, with a polite but perfunctory, "Excuse me," left the room.

Delilah turned to Jimmy, her wrinkled face crinkled with concern. "What did I do, Jimmy?"

"It's not you, Delilah. It's a long story. I think you deserve to hear it. Do you have time for tea?"

"A teatime story suits me just fine."

Delilah listened soberly, sipping her tea while Jimmy shared the story of his marriage to Ariel, and her father's words about her choice of husband. Now he might be dying and Ariel is refusing to see him.

"Ahh, that's why," she said patting the Bible. "Maybe you'd better go check on her. I'll get on home."

"Thank you, Delilah."

"Don't thank me. Thank *Him*." She pointed up and smiled. Jimmy helped her on with her rain gear and opened the door. "Still pissing out there, I see," she said and pushed her way home.

Jimmy found Ariel sitting on the bed, legs stretched out, petting Molly. "Before you say anything, you know my opinion on religion," she said through thin lips.

He sat beside her and took her hand. "I don't think this is religion, Ariel. I think there's something else going on here. My sensei reminds me before every practice that there's more to us than our bodies and brains–something bigger than ourselves that we're connected to."

She stared at him. "What has all this got to do with forgiving my father?"

"This message–if you want to call it that–that Delilah read to you, is–"

"Is creepy, is what it is!"

"It only seems that way because it has come right now when you're struggling. It's a connection thing. A spiritual thing. Not a religious thing. And those words that Delilah read are what you're supposed to do."

"But I *want* to stay mad at him!" she flung out.

"What good will that do you? You've gnawed away at it for years and in the end it will eat you up."

"But why can't *he* apologize to *me*? I didn't have any *evil speaking* or *malice* until *he* started it. Why should *I* have to do all the hard work?" Ariel was digging in her heels. She was loath to relinquish her accumulated resentments.

"Because, sweetheart, you won't find any peace until the breach is mended. I didn't feel any peace until Tan-teck told me why my father sent me to Canada as a baby. Once I knew that, I was able to forgive him. But he was dead by then, and it was too late. I hope that somehow his spirit has picked up my apology."

There was a long period when she said nothing. She stroked Molly, and pouted. Then she heaved her shoulders and sighed. "I know you're right. And now it seems that even St. Paul himself is lecturing me." She paused. "If I went over, do you think you could come with me?"

"If I went over, it would be to visit Tan-teck and Mr. Lim. Not to see your father."

"So *you* don't forgive him, but you want *me* to!"

"That's not the point, Ariel. I frankly don't give a damn how he feels about me. I didn't then, and I don't now. I was just angry that he hurt you."

"I guess I'll have to figure out how to cover up these feelings I've been carrying around."

"Don't cover them up, Ariel. Bury them." He had a feeling the conversation was over and stood up.

Ariel lifted Molly off her lap, got off the bed and wrapped her arms around the love of her life. "There are times when you amaze me. Even after all these years, you'll say something that comes out of nowhere." She broke away and looked him full in the face. "You're a man of mystery, Jimmy Tan."

"Want to do some exploring?" he teased.

She punched him. The phone rang. It was Lana—with news.

Delilah had left the Tan household feeling sadder than she imagined. After shaking out and hanging up her poncho over the bathtub, she sat at the kitchen table. "I tried, Lord. I did my best. I've failed to reach Ariel, just as I've failed to reach my own daughter. Vivien doesn't realize how hurtful her criticisms of me are. At least I *hope* she doesn't. If she does, then that's twice as bad. Maybe she will climb down from her high horse before I kick the bucket. I'll continue to pray for her. And now I'll add Ariel to my prayer list. It's all I can do."

Her tabby rubbed against her legs, purring loudly. "Oh, you want to be on the list, too, Tabitha? Don't you know you're already on there, my little darling? I give thanks for your love and faithfulness every night before I go to sleep." She got up from the table. "Now, what can I feed us?"

Thirty-nine

Miguel and Teresa Flores sat with their guests at one of the crescent-shaped booths, enjoying Mexican coffee, Kahlua and conversation. This was what they loved best about their little business, talking with friends. Kittridge had become such a regular that they thought of him as a friend. And Harlow, who had eaten most of his meals with them for the past five days, had quickly earned a place on the list.

"We will be sorry to see you no more, Henry," Miguel said, his ·round, brown face registering his sadness.

"*Si, si. Es verdad,*" Teresa said.

"And I'll miss you *and* your wonderful food," he replied. I have to say it's been the highlight of my stay. I've been wind-blown, wet and rarely warm, but I could always count on warmth here." He raised his glass and they lifted theirs. "Here's to warmth!"

"*¡Aquí está el calor!*" Miguel echoed.

They sipped.

"And good food," Harlow continued.

"*¡Y por la buena comida!*" Miguel shouted.

They sipped.

"And friendship."

"*Si, si. Y Amistad,*" Miguel cheered.

They sipped.

At this point, Kittridge was hoping they wouldn't find something else to toast or he'd be tottering on his way home. Even the gargantuan meal couldn't sop up all the alcohol. "So, back to the sun, you lucky devil. Wish I was on that plane with you."

"No, you don't, Keith. Even though it can be pretty miserable here, there have been some days that absolutely sparkled. The air is clean and fresh. You never get that in L.A. I'd pick Britannia Bay over L.A. any day."

Miguel nodded. "He is right. We are so happy here. We are grateful to God. We have everything we need. We miss our family only."

Teresa nodded. "*Si, si. Es verdad.* We have many uncles and aunts and nieces and nephews."

"But we are going to visit them at Christmas for two weeks."

"What!?" Kittridge yelped. "You're closing the restaurant? Where will I eat?"

The two of them laughed, knowing that Edith was a good cook. She had often contributed one or two of her dishes to the free lunch for the indigent every Wednesday at whichever church was charged with the event that week. They had seen her in the Catholic church basement and heard comments about her meals.

Harlow cleared his throat. "Well, I'm sorry that I have to break up this wonderful party, but it's time for me to go."

As they slid out of the booth, Kittridge lurched a little. "Whoopsy-daisy," he chuckled. "That last Kahlua seems to have had a little kick to it."

"Maybe another cup of coffee?" Teresa suggested.

"That's a good idea. After we get rid of this Yank, I'll buy a cup."

Harlow held out his hand to Keith. "It's been a real pleasure, Keith."

"Likewise, Hank. Come back any time. I might even give you a job."

Harlow laughed then turned to Teresa, hugging her soft, ample body. "*Muchas gracias por todo.*"

He repeated the gesture with Miguel. Then they slapped each other's backs, pulled away and gripped hands.

"*Vaya con dios, mi amigo,*" Miguel uttered.

"*Muchas gracias.*" Harlow's voice caught.

Keith watched the interchange with a touch of envy. He wished more people demonstrated their heart-felt emotions like that. We're all a bunch of tight asses, he thought.

Harlow picked up his bag, gave a wave and was gone. Keith sat back down. Teresa poured him another cup of coffee. The quiet was deafening.

Forty

Wednesday, November 12th

Ray Rossini's wish for the return of the daily grind was granted. Rotten weather had driven small-time criminals indoors, lulling the squad into a state of ennui. The only ripple of arousal came when Daphne Abernathy crept hesitatingly into the station, clasping her handbag to her chest and asking to see the Police Chief. Giving the reason for her visit, she followed Mary Beth into the chief's office, flinching when the door closed behind her.

Wyatt rose. "Hello Mrs. Abernathy. Why don't you sit down?" He pulled out one of the chairs in front of his desk. She sat on its edge. "I understand you have something you want to show me?"

"Yes. It's a note that was found in the closet after Mr. Nygaard left. It had become stuck in the baseboard." She reached into her handbag and extracted the piece of paper. "It's almost the same colour as the wall, so it was easily missed. It's just that Louise–that's our cleaner–has a keen eye." She held it out to Chief Wyatt. He opened it and read: WATCH YOUR BACK. The generic block letters implied that the sender planned on anonymity.

"Mr. Abernathy wanted me to destroy it, but I couldn't. I thought it was what you call evidence. But anyroad, it doesn't matter now ... now that you've arrested someone."

"Well, just to allay any worries you might have, I doubt whether it would have helped Mr. Nygaard avoid his fate. But thank you for bringing it in. We'll add it to the file." He stood.

She seemed surprised. "That's all?"

"Yes, that's all."

Her body relaxed and the tension left her face. "Oh, thank goodness you don't have to come in and search the premises."

Wyatt smiled. "No."

"And you won't breathe a word of this to Mr. Abernathy?"

So that was why she was on edge, he thought. "No. My lips are sealed." He opened the door and escorted her out to the front door.

Signalling Ray and Jimmy into his office, he showed them the note. "Bring me the list of the show's personnel." Ray brought it in and they ran through the names, wondering who was trying to warn Nygaard. As Wyatt deliberated on what to do with this information, a call came in from Judge Silverman.

"Good morning, Mort." He raised his eyebrows at Ray and Jimmy.

"I've got good news and bad news. Feldman has been denied bail."

"How did he plea?"

"Here's the bad news. Not guilty."

"I'll inform my officers. Thanks for letting me know."

Silverman ended the call without another word.

"Looks like you'll have to get all your ducks in a row," Wyatt said. "Feldman has pleaded not guilty."

"Ah, shit," Ray said. "I wonder what numbskull of an attorney advised him to do that."

"Yeah, that flies in the face of reason," Jimmy said. "Maybe Feldman thinks he's going to get help courtesy of Bibi Benson."

"I wonder who his first phone call went to," Ray speculated.

"I'd guess Allen Benson," Jimmy said.

They were interrupted by Mary Beth's voice on the intercom. "Chief, I just got a call from a friend. Seems that *Paradise Pines* has finished filming here and they're going back to Hollywood."

"Oh, is that so? Thanks, Mary Beth."

"Well, that was fast," Ray said.

They chewed over the information.

"Maybe the doo-doo has hit the fan back in Hollywood. Could be the bad publicity."

"More than likely it's a combination of that and bad weather."

"Whatever, I'll be glad to see their arses out the door," Ray said.

Ariel had been sitting and thinking. And the more she thought, the more muddled her thoughts became. Would Jeffrey be any help? She knew it was early, but he worked from home. There was no reason why she couldn't call him. When he answered, his energetic voice proved he had been up and had at least one cup of coffee.

"How is Kate?" she asked. Not, "How is Dad?" She imagined that her mother's mental state would provide an answer to the unasked question.

"She's doing fine. Dad's back home from the hospital."

"Oh, that's good." Two up. Two down.

"She's pretty well taking care of him. There's help that comes in twice a day to spell her off."

"What kind of help?"

"Rehab exercises to keep him moving. Mom can't do that. He's too big. But she's helping him with his speech. He has aphasia. And they're playing games to stimulate his memory. And the best thing is, it's boosted her self-esteem. Ever since she stopped working, she's felt like a maid. So in a way, Dad's stroke has reversed their positions and now she's the one in charge."

"Hmm. So he's not dying."

"No. He's not dying."

"Okay. Then I don't have to come over." Silence. It was as though the line had gone dead. "Jeffrey? Are you still there?"

She heard a deep sigh. "Yes, I'm still here. You know, Ariel, this would be a good time to come over because more than likely Dad has forgotten what he said about Jimmy. He may not even remember him. In fact, he might not even remember *you*."

The words stunned her. "Does he remember you?"

"Yes, but that's because I've always been in his face."

She recalled the many arguments they had had. No doubt, their intensity had hard-wired the drama into their brains. Later, as she cleaned the kitchen, the topsy-turvy world that was her family sparked something in her. Jeffrey might be right. And Delilah, too. It might be time to see her family again.

Gabriella Rossini was wiping tears from her dark eyes. Lana knew the news startled her former student and one of her favourite friends, but she hadn't expected her to cry. But why not? Gabby had given way to her emotions during her baking classes, often crying over her soggy flans and flopped soufflés.

Lana thought inviting Gabby for tea after school would be the best time to alert her to the possibility that she would be moving to Torino. Perhaps it had been a mistake. After all, there were several months before the move … if it came to that. Why throw caution to the wind? "Gabby, it's not for sure, you know."

"But … I mean, he said he's going to set up a place for you to teach. It sounds like heaven. It's just that I will miss you so much." And that got her sniffles on the move again. But she sighed and straightened up. Then she worked her mouth into a smile. "I'm just feeling sorry for myself."

"Maybe I jumped the gun by telling you. So many things could go wrong."

"Like what?"

Lana smiled at her innocence. "Well, for one thing, he's a romantic. I don't know how practical his plans are. And they may change once he returns to Torino. He may decide it was all a mistake … both me and his cockamamie idea. So I'm afraid to do anything until I know for sure that everything is written in stone."

Gabby shook her head. "But you know, Lana, when Stefano took me under his wing in Pesaro, I thought he was the sweetest man alive. He was like a father to me. And I could tell when you arrived there that he only had eyes for you. He's still like that. I can't imagine him not honouring his word. If he says he loves you and is going to make you happy, I believe him. Why don't you?"

Lana shrugged. "I have men issues."

"Well, get over them," she said abruptly, which got them both laughing.

"Okay, mother."

"There are men, and then there are men. You know what I mean?"

"Yes, I do. And you're right. All I have to do is look at your dad and Jimmy Tan. And even my own father. They're all devoted to their wives."

"So you could be here past the summer?"

"At least."

"I don't know if I can keep a secret that long." But there was a twinkle in her eye.

"Gabby!"

"I'm kidding, Lana. Honestly, I feel privileged that you would share this news with me. Does anyone else know?"

"Just Ariel. I'm afraid to tell anyone else. It's almost like inviting bad luck to say the words out loud."

"Oh, Lana. You sound like a superstitious old Italian."

"Maybe the culture is rubbing off on me."

"If you think it is now, wait until you get to Torino!"

Forty-one

Friday, November 14th

T he rough draft sitting in front of Keith Kittridge had him shaking his head in disgust. *What do they teach kids in school these days? I'll bet Miguel could write a sentence that made more sense than this.* He had agreed to bring in a field study student who wanted to be a reporter. It was giving him a lot of headaches and he wished he had never agreed to it. The kid didn't know basic grammar or proper punctuation. The phone rang as he blue-pencilled yet another misspelled word.

"Kittridge," he answered.

"Hello, Keith."

"Hank! How're you doing?"

"I hope you're sitting down," came the reply.

Kittridge's heart picked up its pace. "What's up?"

"Big article in today's *Daily Variety*. Seems that Bibi Benson has disavowed any ties with Felix Feldman. Cast him off like a filthy coat. And Allen has washed his hands of *Paradise Pines*. Didn't say anything more than 'you figure it out' when he was asked why. Lots of speculation on the grapevine."

"No doubt. Well, how Feldman will get the funds to defend himself without Bibi Benson behind him is going to be a big problem. He's pleaded not guilty, you know."

"Well that's the other news. Feldman's attorney here has requested that he be extradited to Los Angeles to stand trial."

Kittridge whistled. "You don't say. Well, well. Going to be some long faces at the police station. By the by, how much of this can I put in my paper?"

"It's in the public domain, Keith. So go for it."

"Hot off the press, eh? The news sort of dried up once Feldman was arrested. This will generate some revenue. Thanks, Hank."

"Any time. So, how are things in Britannia Bay?"

"Shrouded in mist and rain. It's been pissing down since you left. What about your neck of the woods?"

"The air is as brown as the ground. I'm heading off to Hawaii in a couple of days for a week or so. Gotta get away from the other news-hounds who've been on my tail since I broke the news about Feldman. Going to do some scuba diving, soak up some rays, and snooze a lot."

Kittridge guffawed. "Tough life. Well, have a great time."

"I will. Give my best to Teresa and Miguel. Tell them the food at the El Coyote here isn't as good as theirs."

As soon as he hung up, Kittridge put on his Macintosh and made a bee line for the police station.

Wyatt's surprise visitor piqued his curiosity. "Hi Keith. What brings you out in this deluge?"

Kittridge looked around at the upturned faces in the squad room. He turned back to Wyatt. "Got some info you might be interested in," he mumbled out of the side of his mouth.

Wyatt pointed to his office. After hearing about the extradition request, he knew right away what the reactions of his lead detectives would be.

"Well, shit!" Ray blurted out. "After all our effin work!"

Jimmy's face darkened. His silence spoke for itself.

Kittridge hadn't minded sharing that bit of news with the police, but he kept to himself the explosive details concerning Bibi Benson and her brother. That was strictly for his paper. He knew he'd be testing his friendship with Bill Wyatt, but business was business.

When Jimmy arrived home, Ariel sensed at once that he had not had a good day. He gave her a quick kiss on the cheek, patted Roger on the head and then went to clean up and change. She put the finishing touches on dinner and was glad she had decided on one of his favorites–braised short ribs with mashed potatoes and caramelized onions and carrots. She opened a bottle of red wine.

When she dished out the food, he smiled. "How did you know I had a crappy day?"

"I keep telling you, we angels have our ways."

"Well, this is exactly what I need." He dug in like a starving dog.

They ate in silence for a few minutes, then Jimmy took two gulps of wine and, as was their habit, asked her about her day.

"Never mind mine, honey. It can wait. What happened at the station?"

After hearing his angry rant, she understood the reason behind it. Deep disappointment. "All the work you did to put that case together. It's a shame."

"Well, at least the attorneys down there will realize we're not a bunch of backward cops who don't know a writ from a tort."

"Then you think the extradition request will be granted?"

"No reason for it not to be. His crime falls under the dual criminality treaty. But these things take time. So he'll be a guest of Her Majesty for a while." He finished his dinner, sipped more wine, and pushed his chair away from the table. "So, tell me about your day."

"Eventful, in its own way. If Lana leaving isn't bad enough, Annika told me they're moving to Victoria. Her husband, Zack, got hired by an airline and he's going to be flying again. He's over the moon."

"You'll miss Sara."

"Yes, I will. If we had ever had children, I would have wanted them to be exactly like her."

"Are you regretting our decision, Ariel?"

"God, no! Children grow up and cause you heartache and worry. There's plenty of that in the world without taking on more."

He nodded. "We dodged a bit of it by moving here."

Roger decided that he hadn't had enough affection from his master and took that moment to hop onto Jimmy's lap. "Well, hello there, buddy boy."

Ariel smiled. "Speaking of kids."

Ray was dining with his parents. And, as usual, he felt like a little boy, with his mother making sure he ate every bite and his father doing a running commentary on the superiority of Italian cuisine. The only difference was that he could have a second glass of Valpolicella. Or a third, if he chose. And today, he chose.

"You know, Ray, when Lana goes to Italy, her house will come on the market," Umberto said.

"Yeah. So?"

"We are thinking of buying it."

"Why? You live in a beautiful house now."

"But Lana has a restaurant style kitchen," Silvana said. "It would be perfect for us. We could have our larger celebrations there instead of at Catalani's. This house is too small and so is yours. And if Gabby wanted to practice some Pesaro dishes, she could use that kitchen."

"Has she said she wants to do that?"

"Yes. I think she has her eye on taking over more of the cooking. She said she may want to train someone else to do the baking."

"You mean like Lana taught her?"

"Exactly."

Ray smiled. "Well, that's interesting. By the way, has Lana told you she is leaving?" He poured himself a third glass of wine and drank a third of it.

"Not yet."

"Then aren't you counting your chickens before they've hatched?"

They both shook their heads.

When they said nothing, he became suspicious. "Why not? What do you know?" he demanded.

"Our lips are sealed," Umberto said.

Ray laughed. "Look at the two of you. This whole business about Lana and Stefano has you acting like co-conspirators. I don't even recognize you."

"I didn't hire the private detective," Umberto argued.

"I'll give you that one. But until we know for sure she's leaving, I don't want to hear another word. So, include me out."

"'Include me out'? What kind of English is that?" his father asked.

"What have I told you, Umberto? After three glasses of wine, he doesn't make sense."

Forty-two

Tuesday, November 18th

Wyatt listened to the orders, grunted a reply and ended the conversation. Calling Ray and Jimmy into his office he passed along Judge Silverman's message. "Is your case file in shape to be faxed to L.A.? We just got a request to send it down as soon as possible."

"It is."

"Okay. Let me have a look at it before we do that." After reading the meticulous but dry case notes for about thirty minutes, his eyelids became heavy. Three loud raps on his door and Mary Beth's shouts of "Chief Wyatt!" shook him out of his stupor. He dropped the file and rushed to open the door. He saw his team gathered around Ray's desk. "What's going on?"

"It's *The Bayside Bugle*, Chief," she said, holding out a copy to him. "It's all about Bibi Benson and Feldman. "

"Christ!" he shouted and snatched the issue from her hands. '*Bye, Bye Bibi*,' the headline read. "That idiot!" He called Ray and Jimmy into his office and closed the door. He began reading the article. "Have you read this?" he asked them.

"Most of it," Ray said.

He handed the paper to him. "Finish it. I've got to call Silverman. If Feldman gets wind of this, there's no telling what he'll do."

As it happened, the judge was one step ahead of him. "I'm preparing to have Feldman transferred to a buddy cell. He'll be less likely to try to take his own life if there's someone with him."

"Has the news hit the cells yet?"

"Not yet."

Wyatt exhaled a stream of air. "Thank God for that."

"Yes. He does come in handy, now and then," Silverman replied, with a touch of sarcasm.

Wyatt next called Kittridge, launching right into him. "Kittridge, you numbskull. Don't you realize this information will reach the prison population? Feldman's being moved to make sure he doesn't commit suicide."

"Hmm, that fast, eh?" Kittridge said coolly. "Well, maybe I did him a favour then. And frankly, Bill, I don't give a fiddler's fart about Feldman. He's a murderer, plain and simple."

"But when a prisoner is harmed for any reason it creates a bureaucratic nightmare for us. Can you imagine the headlines then? We'd have the John Howard Society parked on our doorstep, and our streets would be clogged with demonstrators."

"It would sell more papers," he replied laconically.

"I can't believe you!" Wyatt raged. "Is that all you care about? Selling that rag?"

"That rag keeps bread and butter on my table, Wyatt. So, yes, that's all I care about. Now, I'm hanging up before I get angry." And he did.

As Wyatt feared, it had taken a nanosecond for the news to hit the prison's general population, possibly by an employee bringing in a paper. Snide remarks about his girlfriend dumping on him assailed Feldman's ears. His sobbing only served to exacerbate the situation, encouraging endless chants and "boo hoos." When he was escorted from his cell, whistles and catcalls followed him. "Going to miss your sweet ass, homo boy." On any other day he might have had a flippant reply, but today he was wrung out. *How could she do that to me? After what I did for her? There's only one thing for me to do now.*

Lana, Annika and Delilah sat at Ariel's kitchen table enjoying their coffees and the croissants still warm from Lana's oven. It was a cozy scene with the cats snuggled in their corner beds. "Well, girls, it won't be long before Lilah and I will be sitting here by ourselves."

"And with no crescent rolls, either."

"The problem is that they don't freeze well, Delilah, or I'd bake a bunch and leave them for you."

"Oh, that's all right, Lana. I get enough goodies to bring home after church on Sundays. God's message provides the soul food. The parishioners provide dessert!"

"Two good reasons to go," Annika said.

"How is Sara enjoying the picture book of the Bible?"

"She really had fun with the animals going on to Noah's ark. Then I found a video online of The Irish Rovers singing about no unicorns on the ark, and now she sings, 'I just can't see no unicorns' whenever she's searching for something. It's so funny."

"Well, I hope the book helps her remember me."

"Oh, no worries there, Delilah. You're a part of her life that she'll never forget. And you know, we aren't that far away. We'll come back for visits now and then."

"Good. I want to see her growing up."

"I suppose you're in the thick of Christmas rehearsals, Ariel."

"Yes, I am, Annika. Patricia thought we'd do Bach's Christmas Oratorio after the choir got their tongues around German with the Brahms Requiem. But then we couldn't get enough really good musicians to pull it off. And frankly, we thought it was just a bit too difficult for the chorus members. Then we decided on Saint-Saëns Oratorio de Noël. It's a gorgeous piece. Not too large an orchestra and lots of solos, which will give choir members a chance to shine."

"What language is it in?" Delilah wanted to know.

"Latin."

"Why don't you do it in English?"

"Mostly because the translations are so awful," she smiled. "And English really isn't a very nice language to sing in."

"Hmph! It's too high-brow for me. I prefer Christmas carols sung in English."

"We tried giving an all-carols Christmas concert, but people said they expected something grander from our choir. So we went back to the traditional big works."

"It's too bad we won't be here for it," Annika said.

"No problem. We're recording it. I'll send you a link to the site."

"Super. Thanks."

"Oh, Lana. I've been meaning to ask if you were free to spend Christmas day with Jimmy and me."

"Well, as a matter of fact …" and she gave a coy smile. "Stefano and I are going to San Francisco. It's time my parents met him."

"Oh, super!" Ariel said. "They'll love him."

"They'll love him more once I tell them about his family roots. They can be such snobs."

"Yes, but it'll be comforting for them to know you're not being strung along by some phony archduke from a former royal family."

"True. But he's pretty close to it."

"Gosh. Imagine that. We've got an ordinary chef who is anything but ordinary," Delilah said.

"You can say that again." Lana grinned. "Actually, he's extraordinary … if you get what I mean." Her eyes glittered in fun.

The innuendo was not lost on them—not even on Delilah, who chortled along with the rest of them.

Wyatt had finally finished reading the case notes when he received a surprising call from Feldman's court-appointed solicitor. What he heard managed to cheer him up. He was sure Ray and Jimmy would feel the same way.

"Fellas, I've just heard from Feldman's lawyer. He's decided to forego the extradition and to plead guilty. Might've been the DNA from Nygaard's blood that did it. I'm guessing he waited too long to wash his jeans and it set in. The lab couldn't find anything on his jackets, though. So we'll need to ask him about that."

"I imagine Canada not having the death penalty helped persuade him," Jimmy said.

Ray nodded. "And Bibi Benson bailing on him meant no money to mount a legal team in L.A."

"This is a break," Jimmy said. "Maybe now we'll find out what happened."

"When do we get to interview him?" Ray wanted to know.

"Waiting to hear, but it should be pretty soon, I would think." He handed the file to Jimmy. "Good thing I'm a slow reader or these would have been in L.A. by now."

Forty-three

Thursday, November 20th

A stealthy, icy fog had crept in overnight–the kind seen only during the worst days of winter. By the time dawn stole in, it had been usurped by a full-scale gale. It didn't put off off-duty cops from spending a few hours hanging with their mates, however. The anticipated arrival of Felix Feldman had the station air crackling with excitement, and they wanted in on it.

Wyatt, Ray and Jimmy spent the early morning hours conferring, after having had a practice session the previous day. They had fielded every conceivable question. Covered all the bases. Now they trusted their good luck charms to prevent anything from pitching them a curve.

Promptly at ten o'clock, Feldman, in his institutional red T-shirt, sweatshirt and pants, was escorted from the underground garage by two law enforcement officials. Wyatt, waiting at the top of stairs, led Feldman to the "hard" interview room, then joined Novak in the observation booth with his copy of the questions and the case file. Ray, who had been tipped to lead the interrogation, sat opposite Feldman. Jimmy sat in a back corner.

Feldman's lawyer was relieved that Wyatt hadn't manacled his client to the cuff bar on the floor-bolted chair.

The prisoner seemed calm. When the questioning began, he sat up and licked his lips as though preparing for a photo shoot. Early on in the proceedings, he told them Eddie had mentioned that he was seeing Nygaard after the fireworks. He already knew Nygaard had a gun, so when he was helping out with Hallowe'en decorations, he snooped around the house. It only took a few minutes to find it in a drawer beside the bed.

"How did you get the code to enter the house?"

"That was easy. When I was a stage actor, I learned to read the prompter's lips. When I saw Mac mouthing the numbers as he punched in the security code, I watched the next time he did it, and memorized them."

With those roadblocks out of the way, Feldman said he was sure he could carry out his mission to murder Nygaard. It had been a simple thing to slip rohypnol into Mankoff's can of beer.

"What happened when you got to Nygaard's house that night?"

"When he opened the door and saw me, he wasn't happy. He asked where Eddie was. I told him he was in the car on his cellphone and he'd be in soon. He wanted to know why I was with Eddie and I said he had had too much to drink and didn't want to chance getting pulled over. I said I would go back out to the car, but first I needed to use the bathroom. He let me in and I saw a gun in his hand, which scared the hell out of me. But then I realized how lucky I was because I wouldn't have to get it from the bedroom. I asked him what he was doing with the gun. And he looked at it like he'd forgotten it. He told me we were early and he thought a stranger who'd come by earlier and knocked him down had come back. He showed me the bandage on the back of his head. When he started to go through to the hallway, I rushed him from behind. We struggled but he stumbled back. I grabbed the gun and shot him."

"Why did you retrieve the shell casings?"

"I wanted you to think it was a professional hit."

"What did you do with them?"

"On the way back to the motel, I dropped them one-by-one on the road."

"What did you do with the gun?" Ray asked.

"I buried it in a hole under a hedge."

"Where, exactly?"

And when he told them, Ray and Jimmy buried their smiles.

"Why did you turn off the breaker?"

"So the neighbours would think he had gone to bed."

"We found evidence of Mr. Nygaard's blood on the pair of jeans you washed. But where is the jacket you were wearing?"

"It wasn't a jacket. It was a cheap see-through rain poncho. I washed it off. Then I stuck it in a bag and put it in a clothes donation bin."

"Where, exactly?"

He told them. Wyatt made a note to get his constables to a charity shop nearby, but he doubted it would be found with so much rain having people looking for just such an item. "Now, Mr. Feldman, we would like to know what your motive was in killing Mr. Nygaard."

For the first time, the energy that had been carrying him along flagged. He cleared his throat before answering, and took a sip from the water glass. "I was convinced she wanted me to get rid of him." He looked down.

"By 'she,' who do you mean?"

He looked up. "Bibi Benson." His voice cracked. His face crumpled. "I loved her. She was my big sister. She helped my career. Paid for my courses. Made sure I was her makeup man. I would have done any-thing for her. So when she said she wished Nygaard was permanently out of the picture—is how she put it—I knew what she meant. She told me the producers of *Paradise Pines* were looking for a new makeup artist. That the show would be on location in Canada. It would be a perfect opportunity for something to happen to Nygaard. She had her boyfriend, Avi Rothman, arrange to have me hired." He paused. "You know the rest."

"Do you know if Mr. Rothman was aware of why she wanted you on the show?"

"No. I think she duped him, too," he said, bitterly.

"It must have disappointed you to learn that Miss Benson has turned her back on you," Ray said.

In the booth, Wyatt let the invectives fly. They had agreed that there were to be no leading comments.

Feldman's face flushed and he flung out his free hand. "When I heard what the prisoners were saying, I thought they were lying. I couldn't believe she would do that to *me* ... not after what I did for *her*. *She* got what *she* wanted. And now she's left me to rot in prison!" He began to cry. His lawyer took out a small packet of tissues and handed it to Feldman, who whispered his thanks.

Ray realized his error. He waited until Feldman had regained his composure. "Do you have anything more you would like to say?"

Feldman shook his head.

"Then we'll need you to write down the events as they happened."

The lawyer had remained mute throughout the entire interview. It had gone against his better judgment, but when Feldman told him he was changing his plea and not to interfere, he acquiesced fearing for his client's mental health. Ray placed paper and pen on the desk. Feldman began writing. Wyatt left his post. Ray and Jimmy did the same. Novak continued recording.

"Well, Jimmy, you were right," Wyatt said outside the door. "Poor bugger. She's left him swinging in the wind. Figuratively, of course. Now, I'm going to grab a coffee while we wait."

It wasn't long. After roughly forty-five minutes, the lawyer knocked on the inside of the door. Wyatt hurried to open it, Ray and Jimmy in his wake.

"I've looked it over," the lawyer said to Wyatt. "It's complete."

"He speaks," Ray said out of the side of his mouth to Jimmy.

Wyatt entered the room and took the signed confession from Feldman's hand. "Thank you very much, Mr. Feldman."

He nodded.

The two police escorts had spent their time in the kitchen drinking coffee, eating pastries and swapping stories with fellow officers. They now retrieved their charge and left the premises the way they came in.

"May God have mercy on his soul," Mary Beth uttered.

"Kewpie would shit a brick if he knew the gun was buried in his flower garden," Ray laughed.

"Off you go to dig it up, Rossini," Wyatt ordered.

"Why me?"

"Because you goaded him, you ass. We had agreed that there were going to be no opportunities for him to vent. That's going to look like manipulation."

Ray bit his tongue, slunk off to get into his rain gear, and picked up a shovel from the equipment room. Just his luck that it had to be the day the first winter squall stormed the island.

In the incident room, Jimmy was adding the last bit of information to the board when Wyatt strolled in. He took a seat and looked at it. Then he laughed. "Who'd have thought that Peter O'Toole and Richard Burton would figure in a murder case in little old Britannia Bay? It's almost worth keeping that picture up there for posterity. Sure would be a conversation piece."

"Well, I hope it gathers dust," Jimmy said, darkly.

Wyatt nodded. "Yeah, me too. These last two murders have been too close together for my liking." He pointed to the board. "By the way, we never got around to figuring out who sent that warning note to Nygaard."

"That's right. We didn't. It might be the last thing we do on this case."

"God. I bloody well hope so."

Rain had turned into a slushy mess of sleet and hail by the time Ray pulled up at the house. Through the windshield, he spotted a "For Sale" sign in front. That was fast, he thought.

Gordon Greenwood had had his workmen in to repair and paint the offending wall, then got his cleaners to do what he called a "forensic cleaning." Removing it from his rental stock, he placed a sale notice in *The Bayside Bugle* and already had three responses. Eileen was right–the notoriety was attracting prospective buyers.

Ray hunched over and hurried up the driveway, icy pellets bouncing off his cap. Standing on the house's stoop, he surveyed the area Feldman had mentioned. He crossed the strip of grass that ended at Pickell's property line. Along the edge small, gumdrop-shaped shrubs nestled together creating an unobtrusive border–something you would see between neighbours who were on friendly terms. He slowly paced the low hedge looking for something unusual. Within a minute, his eyes fell on an untidy mound of soil, like a cat had done its business and covered it up. He hoped that wasn't what it was. Taking the spade, he turned over the muddy dirt. It wasn't. He fished out an evidence bag from his pocket, slipped on his nitril gloves, and pulled up the gun, dropping it in the bag. After replacing and tamping down the dirt, he surveyed his handiwork. Pickell would be none the wiser. Pity.

Forty-four

Saturday, November 22nd

Wyatt felt a prickle of uneasiness. He sat at his cherished desk, in his favourite chair. Rocking back and forth, back and forth. At any other time, this action would have soothed his soul. But not this morning. He had called Judge Silverman the previous evening with his concerns. Silverman's noncommittal reply left Wyatt wondering what else could be done to keep the prisoner safe. Even though he was certain he had done all he could, in the end he felt powerless, impotent. Fear continued to fester in some unnamed part of him.

Sherilee peeked into the den. "I'm going to hit the mall, Bill. Do you want to come along?"

The very mention of shopping would normally curdle his stomach. Today, though, it seemed like a brainless way to sidetrack his thoughts. He shocked her by saying he did.

"Maybe you'd better bring along a book in case you decide to sit in the car after all," she said, half in jest.

"Naw. I wouldn't be able to concentrate." He got up.

"What's bothering you?" He told her. She hugged him. "I know you don't leave your job at the station, honey, but your life comes first. And think about Silverman. His burden is greater than yours. Today is his Sabbath. Perhaps he'll be praying for divine guidance."

"Okay. You're right. I'll leave him to sort it out with God."

When Jimmy arrived home from the dojo, he found Ariel outside connecting the little heater to the hummingbird feeder. "It's already dropping down to two degrees overnight. I should've had this up sooner."

"I've seen them drinking the cold nectar."

"Yes, they're hardy little critters. Seems like sunshine is only a memory. But they need warmth. Just like we do." She finished her task.

"I need some warm food right about now." As he was hanging up his jacket, she said: "Kate phoned." The words stopped him in mid-motion.

"The old fart has rallied," she informed him.

"So why did she call?"

"She said he wanted me to come over."

"And …?"

"I told her that unless he wants both of us to come over and apologizes to both of us, it was a non-starter. I'm waiting for her to call back with her answer." She ladled out some split pea soup and brought it to the table. "But honestly Jimmy, I'm like you and Rhett Butler. I frankly don't give a damn whether he apologizes or not. It was amazing but I felt no connection to her whatsoever. And it's weird considering she's my mother. She might as well have been a stranger." She placed a baguette and butter beside his bowl, then sat across from him. "Too much time has passed. Too many emotions have been swept away beneath the bridge, along with all the water. Now, I just don't care."

He understood and had no desire to play devil's advocate any longer. There was only one thing left. "Have you tried to imagine how you'll feel when you hear that either your mother or father has died?" He ripped off a piece of bread, slathered it with butter and began to chew.

"Yes, I have. I'll feel a bit sad, like an old acquaintance has passed away. But I can't seem to dredge up those deep feelings of sadness and grief."

He waited for some soup to clear his throat. "Okay, then. But if you suddenly are hit with those deep feelings, you do know that I'll understand. Right? I've been through it. So I won't hold you to what you've just said."

"You know, Jimmy, you're all the father a girl could ever want."

He laughed. "Jeez, Ariel. Don't creep me out!"

Forty-five

Wyatt was going over the duty roster for Christmas holidays when his cellphone buzzed. He was surprised when he saw the name on the display. "Good morning, Mort."

"Bad news, Bill. Our boy decided to take an early exit yesterday."

"Ah, fuck! How in God's name did that happen?"

"All the stars aligned. His cellmate got sick after lunch and went to the infirmary, leaving him alone. There was a shift change and the guard was late getting to his rounds. That gave Feldman just enough time to make a rope from his bed sheet and hang himself. I don't have all the details right now, but it's a royal cockup."

"Shit!"

"He'd been planning it for a while. They found a note written on the back pages of a book he was reading."

"Did they share the contents with you?"

"No."

"But how would a boy from Hollywood know how to make a noose from a bed sheet?"

"Seems he was an Eagle Scout as a kid. He shared a bit of his early life with his solicitor. He has an older brother in the military."

"What about his parents? Are they still in the picture? Did they accept his homosexuality?"

"I don't know about that, but his mother and father are still living in Rancho Cucamonga where he grew up. They're on their way."

"They must be devastated. What a bloody awful thing to deal with."

"Sorry to start your day off like this, Bill."

"Never mind about that. When, or if, you get anymore details, could you please pass them along?"

"Absolutely."

They said their goodbyes. Wyatt went into the squad room. By standing silently, he garnered everyone's attention. He inhaled deeply, then let the air out in a long stream. "I have just received a call from Judge Silverman. Felix Feldman committed suicide yesterday. He hanged himself."

Sharp intakes of breath punctuated the room.

"Holy hell. How did that happen?" Jimmy asked.

Wyatt shared what he had learned from Silverman.

"It's not that big of a surprise," Ray began. "His life would've been hell in the joint, and he knew it. I'm just surprised he had the balls to do it."

"You're talking about someone who murdered a man in cold blood," McDaniel said.

"Right. You got me there," Ray said.

"Will we be learning more?" Novak wanted to know.

"Silverman said he would pass along info to us as he gets it. But we'll probably never get the full story. And he may not, either."

Heads nodded in understanding. When there were no more questions, Wyatt returned to his office. It was a long while before he could return to matters at hand.

Jimmy brought up the case file on his computer and updated it once again. Seeing the words caused him to pause. He wondered if Feldman had spoken to the prison chaplain. Had he made peace with his decision or was his psyche in anguish right to the end? A place that dark frightened Jimmy.

Ray interrupted him. "Suicides make me so damn angry. They don't think about the ones left behind. The people that loved them. The heartache they're gonna cause. I know he was afraid, but maybe his lawyer could've got him into a prison that had more surveillance—something, anything to protect him." His expression turned sour. "And I hope that lawyer of his advised him how to take care of himself."

"Well, if he did, Feldman didn't buy it."

"Nope. He bought the farm instead."

Jimmy pointed to the note on the whiteboard. "Do you want to do a head banging session on who might have written that note? It's the only thing left hanging." He was too late catching his verbal faux pas.

Ray pounced on it. "You mean besides Feldman?"

"C'mon Ray. Don't be so juvenile."

"Okay. Okay. And about the note, I really don't care who wrote it. As far as I'm concerned, the case is closed. Do you really want to waste our time trying to figure out who it was? I know you like puzzles, so maybe you should do it on your own time. It wouldn't be the first time you did that." His expression might have been neutral, but his words were barbed.

Jimmy felt the sting. He knew Ray was still irritated that he had followed a hunch on the last murder that resulted in it becoming a cold case rather than closed. "I just may do that," he said just as neutrally, but with no intention of chasing down a will-o'-the-wisp.

Forty-six

Molokai, Hawaii

Henry Harlow had just towelled off when his cellphone began the theme from "Goldfinger." Thinking it was the restaurant with his reservation confirmation, he was surprised to see the name on the display.

"Good grief, Keith. Is there no place I can get away from you?" he laughed.

"I think you won't mind me interrupting your nap when you hear what I have to tell you."

"Nap? What nap? I just came in from my morning dive. So, am I correct in thinking this is an important call?"

"You think right. Important and tragic. Our boy committed suicide yesterday."

"Oh my God!"

"He changed his plea to guilty, wrote his confession and during a shift change, he managed to hang himself. The news wires won't have picked it up yet, so I thought you would like first dibs."

After listening for a few more minutes, Harlow had enough for a story. "Thanks very much, Keith. Mind you, it's not the kind of news I like to report, but a scoop is a scoop." After a few final words, he ended the call, composed the column, then called his assignment editor.

Britannia Bay

Ariel was inserting eight candles into the cake when Jimmy blew through the door. "Man, that wind is really something. I almost had help walking home." About to shrug out of his jacket, he halted at Ariel's upraised index finger and one-word command.

"Wait."

He bowed. "Yes, my queen. What is your bidding?"

"Oh, you goof," she grinned. "Right now I need you to get Lilah. She might be blown over crossing the street."

"I'm on my way."

Everything was ready. The table looked beautiful. Mauve garden mums and red and orange leaves added fresh sights and smells of autumn to the atmosphere. The crystal and silver sparkled. The cats were locked in the bedroom. She hated to do that, but they could be a nuisance when there were guests. Molly often begged for table scraps.

"Jumpin' Jehoshaphat. That wind nearly took the legs from under me," Delilah said, when they came in laughing. "If I hadn't had Jimmy to hang on to, I might have been picked up and put down in Oz." Her eyes wandered to the table. "Oh, this looks nice. I see you've got five place settings. Who else is coming?"

"Lana and Stefano."

"I finally get to meet him."

"You're not the only one," Jimmy said.

"You haven't met him either?"

"Nope."

"Neither have I," Ariel admitted.

"Really? In all this time you've never laid eyes on him?"

"Well, I have seen him from a distance, but I've never met him."

"That's strange, don't you think?"

"It is, but I think Lana was making sure he was in for the long haul before introducing him to her friends."

"That makes sense, in a way," Delilah said.

The front doorbell rang. "Here they are." Ariel hurried to the door.

Jimmy and Delilah heard not a word of English, but gathered that introductions were being made. He knew that Ariel had more than a smattering of Italian, so he was not surprised. But Delilah whispered to him. "Wasn't that Ariel speaking Italian? Doesn't he speak English?"

"He must. Maybe Ariel is just welcoming him in his own language."

Shortly after, they entered the kitchen, Ariel holding a bouquet of large white lilies in one hand and a bottle of wine in the other. "They come bringing gifts," she said.

The appearance of Stefano struck Delilah dumb. His astonishing good looks and polished finish were a perfect fit for Lana's beauty and style. They were like a pair of window mannequins: both were tall and slim with olive skin and dark eyes. They wore casual but fashionable clothes. Delilah felt like a pigeon among peacocks.

Lana came over to Delilah and kissed her on the cheek. "Hi, Delilah. Happy Birthday."

Stefano stepped forward and held out a small gift-wrapped box. "*Buon compleanno*, Signora."

Delilah thanked him, then suddenly blushed, recalling what Lana had said about his "extraordinariness."

"The lilies are for you, too," Lana said. "They've got little rubber reservoirs on the bottom of the stems, so don't worry about them wilting."

"Well, isn't this wonderful!"

Ariel went to the stove and lifted a boneless pork top loin roast from the oven. Stefano joined her. As they discussed the glaze she would be making, Jimmy opened the wine. A bit of the green-eyed monster clamped onto his heart as he watched a different Ariel so much at ease with a handsome stranger. Lana pulled out a chair for Delilah, sat down next to her and started a conversation. Delilah put a hand on Lana's arm and leaned into her. "Does he speak English?"

Lana smiled broadly. "Yes, he does. Don't worry."

"Good. Then he can sit next to me."

The evening was turning out to be one of the best birthday parties Delilah could recall. Stefano was happy to teach her the Italian words for things that were on the table and some rudimentary phrases as well. When he said, "Prego" she said, "Oh, like the spaghetti sauce." He didn't understand, so Lana explained in Italian. As the evening wore on, Delilah swore his eyes were made of melted chocolate.

"Time for the cake!" Ariel said. "Now, Delilah. I know you don't like anything to do with age, so I've only got eight candles on this cake ... one for every decade you've lived."

Stefano turned to her. "That cannot be correct. You cannot be more than seventy!"

"Oh, go on with you," she said, batting away his words, and giggling.

"But you are so youthful. Such spirit. You are remarkable."

"And you're full of beans."

Again, Stefano looked quizzically at Lana, who did her best to explain the idiom. He laughed and turned back to Delilah. "*Si, si.* I am Signore Cannellini."

Ariel interrupted the jollity. "I'm going to light the candles now. Don't forget to make a wish, Delilah."

Tucked up in bed, Ariel and Jimmy—and the two cats—discussed the evening, the cats vocalizing their displeasure at being left out of the celebrations.

"Delilah was totally smitten by Stefano, wasn't she?" Ariel said, starting to fade.

"Yeah. He gave her the kind of attention that Italian sons give their mothers until the day they die. When he got up and poured the sparkling apple juice into her glass like a real Italian waiter, the look on her face was priceless."

"You seemed to warm to him, too. "

"He's a genuine kind of guy."

"Mm-hmm." She yawned.

Jimmy decided this was the time. He murmured into her ear, "*Vieni qui, moglie.*"

"What?" she laughed. "Did you get Stefano to teach you that?"

"I thought it was better than fork, knife, and thank you. Something I could really use. So, come here, wife."

"Oh, you're ridiculous. You sound like a caveman."

"Well, how about this? *Vieni tra le mie braccia.*"

"Oh, good accent. How many times did you have to practice that one?"

"Never mind. Just shut up and come into my arms, wife."

Across the street, Delilah softly snored as Tabitha wheezed away on the adjacent pillow. On the kitchen table, a vase of fragrant lilies vied in beauty with a pair of Fratelli Orsini red leather, cashmere-lined gloves. They were the perfect gift. Now, if only her wish would come true. It hadn't been for herself, but for Ariel–that she and her family would mend the rift between them.

Forty-seven

Saturday, November 29th

The wind had flown elsewhere, leaving a shower in its wake. It fell weakly and endlessly, too soft to waken Ariel, but not the cats nor Jimmy who were busy with their breakfasts. Jimmy had emptied the dishwasher and was working on the cryptic crossword when Ariel finally sauntered in. She kissed Jimmy on the top of his head. "Good morning, *marito.*"

"Hmm. I'm guessing that's husband."

"Uh-huh." She yawned, and opened a cupboard for a clean bowl. "Oh, you've put away all the dishes. You darling." Before going to the fridge, she looked out the patio doors. "What a dismal day. Are you off to the dojo as usual?"

"Yep. What are you going to do?"

"I thought I'd take a stab at an anagram of Berens Nygaard's name. I'll save the crossword puzzle for later on. And I'm going to try a new recipe for dinner that Stefano gave me. So that should keep me occupied."

"No singing?"

"Frankly, I don't have the energy. Late nights and too many glasses of wine aren't conducive to singing."

"Doesn't seem to bother the Italians."

"You're right. And they smoke, too. I don't know how they do it."

"Years of training."

She snickered and shook out her muesli, adding fruit and berries and soy milk, then sat across from him. The cats were cuddled together. "Would you look at that? Molly is in with Roger."

"I think it's the weather. You know ... needing more warmth. Just like those little hummingbirds."

"I hope it's not a sign of infirmity."

"Siamese live a long time, Ariel. And she's got a great life. Don't worry."

He went back to his puzzle.

"I think I'll start on that anagram while I'm eating." She got paper and pen and settled back down.

Ray had sheets of paper scattered on the dining room table when Georgina walked by. She turned around and came back. "What are you doing in here? And what's with all the paper?"

"I'm trying to solve a mystery."

"Didn't you just do that?"

"This is part of it. It's not what you'd call evidence, but it might've had a bearing on the case."

"What is it?"

"Someone left a note for Nygaard. It was written in block letters." He held up his reasonable facsimile. She read out the words.

"And you don't know who left it?"

"No. I'm trying to figure it out by a process of elimination. I've got the names of the cast and crew and a print out of their interviews."

"But why, exactly, are you doing it? It's a lot of unnecessary work. You usually leave a case in the dust once it's solved."

He cleared his throat and took another sip of coffee. *How was he going to justify this?*

She grinned. "Let me guess. It has something to do with Jimmy, doesn't it? You're competing with him again."

"Well dammit, Georgie. He always seems to find some needle in the haystack, and he leaves me looking like a local yokel."

"So you're going to try to find this mystery person before he does."

He shrugged his shoulders. "That's the plan."

"Don't do it, Ray. Forget about Jimmy. Just enjoy your free time."

"Without baseball, I don't have any other diversions."

She waited a moment before suggesting one. He threw down his pencil and followed her to the bedroom.

When Jimmy returned from his workout, Ariel was busy at the stove. Spices lined the counter and the pungent smell of chopped garlic filled the room. The piece of paper with permutations of Berens Nygaard's name stared up at him from the table. In bold letters at the bottom was the perfectly apt anagram.

Epilogue

Los Angeles

Tiffany Blair was putting the finishing touches to her make-up when her mother called out from the kitchen. "Tiffany! Come here right away!"

"In a sec, Mom." She first applied setting spray to her face. "What is it?"

"Look what's on the front page of the *Herald's* entertainment section." She handed the broadsheet to Tiffany. After glancing at the headline, Tiffany sat down and read the report. "This is dreadful, Mom. Just awful. First Nygaard is murdered, then Allen quits, and now this. How is this production ever going to survive all the scandal?"

"Are you back on the set on Monday? Maybe you'll find out then."

Tiffany reflected for some time. "I wouldn't be surprised if Bibi put him up to it. Maybe hinted that she wanted her husband out of the picture and poor puppy Flix figured he would help her out."

"Honestly, Tiff," her mother said, gazing at her daughter. "You're writing too many murder mysteries. It's messing with your mind."

Ignoring her mother, she squinted at the ceiling and pattered on. "After he does the dirty deed and is arrested, she gives him the old heave-ho. Where does that leave him? Out on that well-worn limb all by himself. No one to turn to. No help. At the mercy of vicious thugs in the slammer. So what else can he do but do himself in?"

"That's what I mean. It's just another story to you."

"A tragedy, Mom. A good old fashioned tragedy."

Later in the day, as her mother took her regular nap, Tiffany thought about the events. She hadn't wanted Nygaard murdered ... just replaced. After he ignored her script suggestions, her plan was to irritate him with interruptions. When that didn't work, she took advantage of his confusion, memory loss, and signs of paranoia. The note was simply an attempt to increase the pressure on him, get him to quit. How was she to know Felix would kill him? It wasn't her fault.

Acknowledgments

I am deeply grateful to Ruth Findlay for her impeccable reading of the first draft, correcting my errors and omissions and making cogent suggestions, all of which I followed. And a huge thank you to Jim Bartlett, cover designer for the two previous Britannia Bay Mystery books, for stepping in to create the front cover for *Deadly Direction*. To my many supporters, your encouragement has motivated me to carry on. Blessings to you all.

To my Readers: If you enjoy anagrams, you may want to rework Berens Nygaard into something that would suit the story. Should you wish, you may send your solutions to me through the contact page on my website: www.sydneypreston.com

Also on my website are detailed backgrounds of the central characters, which help in understanding them. Book one of the series, *Too Late for Redemption*, touched on them, but for brevity's sake, I did not include them in book two, *Tone Dead,* nor in *Deadly Direction*.

About the Author

Sydney Preston has used her experience working in the television industry in Hollywood and Rome for the framing of Deadly Direction. A classically trained vocalist and avid gardener, she lives in Qualicum Beach, British Columbia—the imaginary village of Britannia Bay—with her long-haired black cat, Lulu. Sydney is also the author of *Too Late for Redemption* (self-published, 2018) and *Tone Dead* (self-published, 2021), books one and two in the *Britannia Bay Mystery* series.

For reviews and more information about her books, please visit www.sydneypreston.com.

CPSIA information can be obtained
at www.ICGtesting.com
Printed in the USA
BVHW082145130822
644508BV00001B/27